Only My Horses Know

(Hope and Horses #1)

Cinda Jo Bauman

Editor-911 Kids

Cover design by: Cinda Jo Bauman

Printed in the United States of America

Published by:
Editor-911 Books
PO Box 313
Eureka, MO 63025-0313
https://www.editor-911.com

DEDICATION

For my daughter, Brittany,
even as a little girl, you always had faith in me.
Some of my favorite memories are of you helping me
with story ideas in the car on the way to school.
I love you so much!

CONTENTS

CHAPTER ONE

*G*od, *please let Momma be better today. She's been sleeping all the time. I'm starting to feel like an orphan.*

I complained my way down the stairs, guessing I would be doing morning chores again. Momma did the morning chores. I did the evenings. It had always been that way—at least until the last couple of weeks.

The sound of Grandma's creaky, old rocker stopped my complaining. There sat Mom, slightly rocking and sipping a cup of coffee. Her long, curly hair was pulled up in a mess of red snarls on top of her head. Dark circles shaded her eyes, making her fair skin look as pale as a cold winter moon. Seeing her out of the bedroom made me almost forgive her for not coming to the barn last night to meet the new horse, the horse that I prayed would wake up the trainer in her and pull her out of her bedroom.

I knelt next to the rocking chair and whispered, "Momma, you okay?"

"Just tired, Kylie."

I smoothed my mom's hair. "The horse got here last night. Remember? The one you're supposed to have trained by September? You'll never guess what his name is."

Mom glanced up but said nothing.

"It's Dragonfly! Isn't that a strange name?"

She nodded.

"Are you hungry, Momma? I could make you something." I waited a bit then moved right in front of her. "How about some more coffee?"

With a slight smile, she shook her head.

"I wish you'd come out with me to meet Dragonfly. He's got big-time issues. Remember that mustang Mr. Riley hired you to train last year? He was such a problem. Dragonfly might be worse."

"We'll see, Sunshine."

I messed in Momma's hair a while, working out some of the tangles before I hugged her and then left to start the morning chores. At the kitchen doorway, I turned. "I think the horses miss you." *And I miss you. Why can't I just tell her?*

Mom looked at her coffee, so I put on my boots at the back door, grabbed my old worn-out gloves, and then headed for the stable. Mom used to find some

2

barn work or just come and hang out with me while I did my chores. She used to ask about the latest adventures with my best friend, Joey. Not anymore.

I needed fresh air to help wake me up—like the sweet Montana mountain breeze that Dad always talked about. But instead, I got a blast of hot, summer yuck. Even the twisted red poppies planted on the sunny side of the barn looked hot and thirsty.

After feeding the horses and mucking stalls, I guided the wheelbarrow, spilling over with straw and manure, to what I called the poop-pile behind the barn. The sound of a familiar whistle made me turn to see Joey riding up on his bike. Riding wheelies must have made him feel taller because I hardly ever saw him on two wheels anymore.

"Hey, grab your bike, and let's hit the trails," Joey said when he came down from his wheelie and stopped beside me.

"I can't. Got a new horse. I watched him a long time last night, and the poor thing never even looked at me." I tipped the wheelbarrow up and tried shaking the mess onto the pile. "Let me dump this, and then you can come meet him."

"You've trained a million horses. He'll still be here when we get back. Come on; one race–I win–we're done."

"You win? You wish. Here, look. His name's Dragonfly." I tucked the empty wheelbarrow against the inside wall of the barn as Joey popped another wheelie and rode it inside, stirring around the straw dust.

He stopped next to one of the stalls in the back of the stable and hooked his arm over the stall door. "Yep, it's a horse. Now, let's go." Pushing off from the stall, Joey rode in a small circle in the aisle.

"Stop that! You're filling the place with dust. And it's not just a horse." I wished I could explain the real reason I was so anxious about Dragonfly. This horse may save my mom. For now, though, I kept my worry over Mom to myself.

Joey would not let up until finally, I threw up my arms and said on the way outside, "All right, already! One quick race. Then you'll have to entertain yourself 'cause I've got work to do."

I wanted to add, *someone has to do it because Mom sure isn't.* But I kept that to myself, too, because what could Joey do about it anyway?

CHAPTER TWO

So much for a quick ride! An hour later, I climbed the muggy trail, swatted at a swarm of gnats hovering around my face, and thought how everything seemed to irritate me lately. "Crap, Joey. Next time, will ya crash closer to the house?" My curls, damp with sweat, slipped from my ponytail and dangled in my eyes. He just had to pick today to crash his bike into a tree. I sure felt my lack of sleep now.

"What are you complaining about? You're not the one hopping up this hill with one leg bleeding into your stupid shoe." Joey pulled off his t-shirt, tied it around his calf, and grumbled something about his bike. Joey seemed pretty upset.

"I'm kidding. You ready to go a little farther?" I asked.

Thanks to lifting bales of hay and hoisting saddles, I was pretty strong for a twelve year old. Good thing, since I'd practically carried Joey up the trail to keep the weight off his messed-up leg. After he nodded, we inched our way up the rest of the trail, leaving my bike and what was left of his dirt bike crumpled behind us.

The midday sun pieced through the Douglas-fir trees, shining down in speckles on the path. I'd lived on this Montana ranch since I was born, so I knew every inch of this trail like I knew every possible way to bug Joey. After the next two curves, the trail would straighten before reaching the edge of the woods.

"Is your mom home?" Joey asked.

"She was just barely awake when I started chores." *And still is if she's like she's been all week.* The thought of Joey seeing how Mom had been looking all week made me cringe.

Finally, we reached the edge of the paddock, cut behind the barn, and then I left Joey to hurry for the house.

"Momma!" My shout broke the silence of the old farmhouse. "Where are you?" I found her upstairs in bed, buried under a blanket heap. "Joey's bleeding all over his face. And his leg—I need help."

"I'm trying to sleep, Kylie. You know where the Band-Aids are."

Mom's stale morning breath slapped me in the face, even though it was well past noon.

"A Band-Aid? This is not a Band-Aid kind of bleeding," I said, as Mom rolled away from me and groaned.

"Then go get your dad." She grabbed a pillow to cover her head.

"But Daddy's down the lane in his shop."

Mom reached for another pillow to completely cover herself.

I clenched my teeth to keep from smarting off and figured the shop was my only choice. When I burst out the front door, I nearly trampled Joey, as he reached the top step of the porch. He had a bloody t-shirt covering the skin torn from his left shin and knee, hair sticking out, and a big, fat lip. I tossed him my bandana wrapped over a bag filled with ice. "Here, use this."

"Why are you throwing things at me?" Joey muttered.

"It's for your lip, *Joe.*" He hated to be called that, so I made sure he heard it. "It's bleeding all down your chin."

We'd been neighbors and shared the same grade at school for years. Picking on each other was what we did best. But when I caught how mean I had just sounded, I took a breath, and said, "Here, sit down before you fall over. I'm going to get Dad."

"I'm fine. I'll come with you." Joey inhaled a pained hiss when he took a step.

I thought maybe annoying him would take his mind off the pain. "You're not gonna cry now, are you?"

"If you're trying to be funny, you stink at it. Help me back down these steps."

After watching Joey limp to the edge of the steps and seeing the pain in his expression, I took the bandana and carefully dabbed at his lip. "Just wait here, and hold this on your lip. Okay? I'll take the four-wheeler and be right back."

Joey grabbed it from my hand. "Cut it out! I said I'm fine!"

I ignored him, like most times, and took off to get Dad. On the way to the shed, I worried about Mom lying in bed on a beautiful day, not caring about a new horse to train or Joey, her favorite person ever. A few weeks ago, she'd have had a fit over Joey being hurt. *See, God, I told you she's acting weird. Why wouldn't she just get up to look at him?*

"He's bleeding? How bad?" Dad asked me after I explained why I was driving so fast that I had to skid into the shop.

"Well, he's not dying or anything like that. But you might think so to look at his pitiful self."

When Dad and I returned, Joey waited in the car while I called his parents. I could hear Dad upstairs talking to Mom, quietly at first, but his voice got angry right before the bedroom door slammed. The sound of his steps rushing down the stairs made me turn away and concentrate on the phone call.

Soon, we were headed to get Joey's father from down the road; then we would travel six more miles to the nearest town. My grandma Hannigan used to call it a "quaint" town. Mostly just had a small grocery store, schools, the post office, and what we needed now—Dr. Jordan's office.

I looked at my dad, grease smudged on his cheek and caked under his nails, and I wished he didn't work so hard at his equipment repair business in the shop. Right now, it was full of equipment the ranchers and farmers had brought over for him to fix.

"Mr. McLagan said he'll be watching for us," I told him.

"Good." Dad glanced back at me a few times between watching the road. Was he wondering if I heard him arguing with Mom? I was glad when he turned his attention to Joey, "So, what happened?"

"We were racing down Noah Trail on bikes. I was winning," I bragged.

"Yeah right, Kye! I would have won—if I hadn't hit that tree root when I tried to pass you. Besides, he's asking me." Joey went on. "My handlebars started shaking, and my feet came off the pedals. Next thing I knew, Kylie was yelling for me. She better not try telling you I was crying. I wasn't crying," Joey rambled, glaring at me.

"You? Never." Dad agreed, then winked at me in the rearview mirror.

"You should see my new bike," said Joey.

"Pretty bad shape, huh?"

"I'll say. He left out the part where he smashed into a tree," I added.

"Yeah, well, maybe I'll win a new dirt bike. I heard Mr. Riley's giving one away as a prize at the Winter Rodeo this year," said Joey.

"Sorry, but I'm winning the dirt bike. I'm not about to let Olivia beat me in barrel racing again this year. Every time I see her, she has to remind me how I *almost* beat her."

Olivia could be so annoying. I always tried to be nice to her. We'd gone to school together since she moved here from Chicago in first grade. But it wasn't easy. At all.

My thoughts drifted to this morning. Did Dad even notice that I was doing Mom's work? Were they arguing about that, and how she didn't even seem to care that Joey was hurt?

CHAPTER THREE

The trip to town took most of the day. By the time we got home, it was time for chores again. The horses lifted their heads when I entered the stable. When they heard the feed bucket clank into the wheelbarrow, their shuffling hooves quickened, and they neighed and grunted at their gates. Dragonfly was facing the corner of his stall with his ears pinned back and his tail tucked between his hind legs. He flinched when my boot accidentally thumped against the gate. I tried everything I knew to calm him, or even just to get his attention, but that sad, jumpy horse just ignored me. He was just like Momma.

"It's okay, Dragonfly," I said as gently as I could to the quarter horse.

He turned his head just enough, so I could see a thin stripe between his eyes, running down almost to his nostrils.

"You're gonna be just fine. Before long, you'll be hanging with all the horses at our ranch, and you won't ever want to leave." Right then, my horse, Kiwi, nickered from her stall in the front of the barn. Now there was a horse that understood everything.

"Momma should come meet you tomorrow. She's the-best-ever trainer in this part of Montana. Well, she was anyway. Lately, she's done more sleeping than training." As I rambled on, the splotchy-brown horse just stood with his nose pushed into the corner like he'd been doing. "But, that's gonna change, huh, Dragonfly? And you're gonna help." Mom was always up for a challenge. I smiled as I hoped that this horse was just what she needed.

Mom's horse, Josie, snorted at me and tossed her head up and down.

"Hey, girl. Did you miss me today? What's the matter? You hungry?" I spoke softly to the black and white Paint. Josie eyed me then pawed the ground and nosed her empty food bucket.

"You miss Mom, don't ya?"

Josie raised her head to look at me.

"Yeah, me too."

I dumped a can full of grain into her bucket, then pet Josie's forelock. Mom once said, "Josie is God's masterpiece," because her mane was split black and white and hung over her mostly black face, except one white patch on her jowl and a white chin. I pressed my cheek to her beautiful face and then moved down the aisle to the next stall.

The outside of this stall was decorated with my trophy and ribbons. The creamy colored mare waited patiently. "Kiwi, how are you? Hungry? Boy, what a day I had. And Momma, I'm not sure anymore what's wrong with her. What do you think it is?" On the wall inside, high enough so Kiwi couldn't chew them, were framed pictures of Mom, Dad, and me after every rodeo at Mr. Riley's ranch. I remembered the day of each photo. In one, Mom and I both had the idea to push Dad's hat over his face, right before the camera clicked.

I squeezed passed Kiwi and stepped up on the side railing to get close enough to the photo to see the sparkle in Momma's eyes and her mouth open while she laughed. I leaned against Kiwi for a minute, closed my eyes, and could still hear her laugh. Mom had volunteered to be a rodeo clown, and she still had a few white makeup smears on her face in the picture. "Oh well, let's get you fed, and I'll come back and tell you all about Joey." Kiwi headed for her bucket and stood quietly.

I worked my way through all nine stalls. I left them each with a can of grain, two flakes of hay, and fresh water in their buckets from the hose. I moped back down the aisle toward the door, running my hand over the top of each gate, thinking about Mom. My fingers jerked back when Kiwi startled me by nibbling them with her soft, damp lips. I had forgotten all about returning to talk to her. Kiwi had not. She tossed her head up and back toward her stall as if to say, "Come on in, and tell me all about it."

I pulled a stool over to Kiwi's stall. "Okay, I'm back. Sorry about that. You should've seen what Joey did to his lip today. Doc stitched it up, and he let me come in and watch! Mom, she was too busy sleeping to help. Can you believe that?" I lay my arms over the gate and slumped against it. "You know how Mom's always teasing Joey's mom about wanting to adopt him. Not today. She just didn't care. That's how she's been lately, like she doesn't care about nothin'."

Kiwi's tail swatted a fly on her hindquarter.

I shifted on my stool, turning away from Kiwi. "Not even about me." I picked threads from the knee of my torn jeans. Kiwi sniffed the air around my head. "Bet you smell the new horse. Don't you go getting jealous; he's only here for a while. And boy is Mom gonna earn her money on that one. That is, if she ever gets out of bed to work her training magic on him. Just between you and me, he's a mess."

When I finished, I secured the barn behind me. The sun had lowered, and Dad must have finished the four-wheeler he'd wanted to work on because a trail of dust followed him up the lane. He zipped past me wearing his favorite wrinkled motorcycle t-shirt and then spun a donut.

"Showoff! Done already?" I asked, shaking my head and thinking he was just as bad as Joey.

"Didn't take long. It just had a bad spark plug wire. Thought I'd go see if Mom's hungry."

"Good luck. She barely looked at me this morning. And then, well, you know about this afternoon." I looked down and kicked some mud off my boot. "I'm sorry if I made you guys fight."

"You didn't. I'm sorry you heard. It wasn't really a fight. It's just she's been sleeping a lot...too much. I'll try to be more patient; and before we know it, she'll get back to her old ornery self." He climbed off the four-wheeler and kicked at some rocks on the lane. "She's been this way before. You probably don't remember."

"She doesn't care about the horses anymore. She's stopped training; that's her job." Under my breath I added, "Not mine."

My eyes swept back toward the house where Dad was looking. I wasn't sure he even heard me. "What if something's really wrong?"

Dad swatted me on the butt with his gloves. "You worry too much, kiddo. I'm sure this will pass. You just keep doing a little more to help her out, like you've been doing. I'll see you inside."

A little more? I didn't expect Dad to help. I knew his job kept him busy, and horses were not his thing, but I'd been doing *a lot* more.

When I came inside, I saw where Mom had tried to start supper. Now she sat in the dining room with Dad while he read the newspaper.

Mom's words came out slow and weak as she motioned toward the kitchen. "I've got to go lay down. Finish that up. Will you guys?"

"But I wanted to tell you about Dragonfly," I said.

"Maybe later."

"Why don't you stay here while we finish, so Kylie can tell you about the horse?" Dad asked.

"Tell me tomorrow, Kye. Okay?"

I'm not sure why she asked me if that was okay because she was already heading to her room.

Dad looked at me and shrugged his shoulders. "Come here, and help me up, will ya?"

I knew this trick, but I took his hands anyway and tugged as hard as I could.

Just when he was about to stand up, he fell back and pulled me down into the chair next to him. "How hungry are you? If you peel a couple potatoes, I'll start frying."

"Okay. Deal." I sat there all squished next to Dad, wondering if he knew what was really wrong with Mom.

After supper and a bath, I lay in bed looking out the window at the stars. The moon glowed a mixture of gold and pink. Between two of the tall pines, I saw the silhouette of the majestic Crazy Mountains of Montana. My hands covered my ears when I thought of Dad's angry voice earlier and of Mom's soft sobs I'd heard this week.

"Lord, is it my fault? Did I do something? Please be with my momma." I prayed, drifting off to sleep. I pried my eyes open and added, "And thanks for keeping Joey from getting hurt too bad today. And thanks for Dragonfly."

CHAPTER FOUR

The sun beat on my cheek. I rolled out of bed and pulled down the shade. On the way back, I tripped over my books, kicked the video game player, and caught my toe in the strap of my sports bra. "Crap!" I grumbled, then flopped back into bed.

"Hey, Sunshine," Mom said quietly from the doorway.

I sat up, grinning. "Mornin', Momma!"

She yawned then said, "I'm going back to bed. Do the dishes after breakfast, will ya?"

"Sure. Don't you wanna eat something with me? I'll cook."

"No thanks, hon." A smell like the school locker room lingered in the air after she shuffled down the hallway, shoulders drooping.

I fell to my pillow, closed my eyes, and listened to the second-hand peck around the alarm clock on my bedside table. For two nights in a row, I'd barely slept. Seemed every hour I'd wake up and check the clock, wishing I could stop the same thoughts from spinning inside my head. My thoughts were about Momma and how much I'd been missing her. My thoughts wondered how somebody could be here and gone at the same time. They planned how working with Dragonfly would remind Momma how she had always dreamed of starting a training center for rescue horses, and she'd be like her old self again.

Dragonfly, Dragonfly, Dragonfly. Momma, Momma, Momma. Around and around, all night long. I thought about how sad the new horse was—and odd—just like his name, Dragonfly. Who would name their horse after a bug?

I remembered the unfinished laundry from last night, so I headed for the dryer, wondering how Mom used to keep up. I just got one load folded, and that stupid basket was spillin' over again. Downstairs, I shook the wrinkles from my Wranglers while picturing Olivia in her tight fitting, low riding jeans. Not me. I can see me squatting down, brushing Kiwi with my crack hanging out. No thanks! I'm not sure how she even got up on her horse, let alone beat me at the race.

Ever since Joey brought up the Winter Rodeo, I'd felt anxious. Kiwi's a great barrel racer; we just needed to work on her strength, so she'd be faster, and then I was sure we'd win.

I paused at Mom and Dad's bedroom door, holding the basket of folded laundry. Mom lay on the bed staring at the ceiling. Junk covered the dresser. Dirty tissues covered the floor on one side of the bed. Dad's pile of laundry from last week had not been put away.

My grandparents had died before I was born. They gave this house to my mom and dad. Grandma loved horses, and she taught Momma everything she knew about training. I wondered what Grandma would say if she were here and saw Momma sleeping when the house was messy, and there were chores to do. I looked at Mom and shook my head. *You used to be a neat freak. I'm so tired; please come back.*

Later that morning, after the usual routine of feeding horses and cleaning stalls, I stopped to see Kiwi. "I know we should train today, but want to take me for a little ride instead? I sure could use one. That Dragonfly tried to keep me out of his stall, turned his fanny at me. Then, when I let him know that wouldn't scare me and squeezed in there anyway, he trembled and swayed back and forth until he had me almost pinned against the wall!" I brushed Kiwi's bangs to the side. "I think Mr. Dragonfly's gonna take a lot of work. That's what I think. I told Mom she might want to start him soon. You know what she said? She said, 'There's plenty of time. He's getting settled in.' Ugh, if she'd come see him, she'd know that Dragonfly is a mess, and he's gonna need every day she's got to get him trained!"

Kiwi pranced in her stall, while I heaved the saddle onto her back. As usual, her sides bloated just as I reached beneath her for the end of the cinch strap. I tugged the front and back cinch snug around Kiwi's belly, then moved to her head and took hold of the reins, close to the bridle.

"I know what you're doing. You can't fool me. Now let out that air, so I can tighten your saddle." I clicked my tongue on the roof of my mouth, signaling her to step forward, while keeping my eyes on her side. Satisfied Kiwi had exhaled, I stepped back to further tighten the cinch. "There we go. Can't have me riding sideways from a loose saddle."

I scribbled a note on the chalkboard in the tack room in case someone came looking for me.

"Took Kiwi. Went to Joey's. Be back later. Love, Me."

I trotted Kiwi first toward the back of the house, where a trail has worn between our property and the McLagan's. On my left, I caught a whiff of the yellow and violet summer wildflowers covering the paddock. To my right, the dense woods shaded the path. It was well over a mile ride to the McLagan's, and the trail rode smooth enough to give Kiwi her rein.

I pulled the band from my wrist and put up my hair into a high ponytail, then wrapped the reins around my hand, leaned down close to her neck, and tightened my knees against her broad chest. Guilt crept over me, like the morning mist over the hills. "I don't know,

Kiwi. Maybe I should stay home and try and get Mom up to eat?"

Kiwi's hooves stomped the trail, ready to run.

Looking back at the house that seemed to have sadness oozing from the windows and doors, I sighed and said, "I gotta get away from here, just for a little while." With my boot, I nudged Kiwi's ribs. "Yah! Come on, baby. Let's fly!" We tore down the path, dust flying behind. The wind in my face blew away my frustration with Dragonfly, and for a moment, I didn't worry about Momma.

The shed door at Joey's stood wide open. That's where he'd be. Like my dad, Joey favored tinkering with motors over messing with the horses, although he did enjoy riding with me now and then. His golden retriever ran toward me as I tied Kiwi beside the shed.

"Hey, Rusty! How's my sweet boy? Did I just see you limping? Huh, Rusty ol' boy?" I bent down and cupped his grey muzzle in my hands.

Rusty's age had not affected his sweetness. He looked into my eyes while we walked to the shed. His tail wagged, and he smiled his doggy smile.

I heard the push broom working its way toward the open door. Dust clouded the air. I backed up against the outside wall and waited for Joey. When the broom pushed the dirt outside the door, I jumped in front of it and yelled, "Wazzzuuuppp?!"

Joey jumped back, dropping the broom. His pale blue eyes bugged out in shock.

I fell to the ground, holding my ribs from laughing so hard. "I got you, Joey! I thought you were gonna crap right on the floor!"

"Dang, Kylie! Wasn't the other day enough for you?" Joey yelled, reaching for his lip to make sure he hadn't made it bleed. "You're lucky I'm so sore everywhere 'cause I'd tackle your butt. We'd just see who was left laughing!" He leaned down to give Rusty's ears a good scratching. "Rusty ol' boy, you forgot to warn me! Some watchdog you are."

Joey suggested a ride to our secret fort on the four-wheelers. I couldn't think of a better way to cheer me up. I tied Kiwi to a tree on the shady side of the shed, where the grass was tall for her to munch. "We'll be back in a while, Kiwi."

As always, we were careful to put Rusty in the pen before we left, and then we parked the four-wheeler and walked the last bit, so not to make a path to be spotted.

The secret fort had been there for two summers. It had changed a lot though. Joey and I scavenged lumber to add to it whenever we could. The fort lay deep in the woods, away from all the family trails for riding, training horses, and four-wheeling. Inside, there were old, moldy-smelling pillows, folded up chairs, and some boxes propped up as a makeshift table for the Monopoly game. Sometimes, a puzzle, half-worked, covered the table. Other times, card games abandoned for another adventure lay around. Stacks of books and comic books covered the floor. Most days, we just hung out on pillows and read and talked.

Last year, Joey had talked his dad into buying some heavy plastic sheeting for a school project. There really was a project, and clear plastic wrap would probably have worked fine. But we were tired of things inside the fort getting soaked in the summer rains. The heavy plastic worked well to cover the roof and line the floor, curling up the sides of the simple framed walls we had built.

"Slow down! What's your hurry?" Joey asked.

"Why are you such a slow-poke?" I turned and looked at him from the tops of my Irish eyes, as Dad called them, ready to start our teasing battle. Instead, seeing the scrapes and bruises from yesterday, I decided to give him a break, just this once.

Pine branches camouflaged the fort. A reflection on the ground caught my eye. I bent to pick up a candy bar wrapper. "You pig. You ate my last Milky Way!"

"Did not!" Joey came back.

"Oh yeah, it just unwrapped itself and jumped out here," I grumbled as I unblocked the secret door.

"Seriously, Kylie, I haven't been out here since we played Monopoly on Tuesday."

"Yeah, yeah, sure," I teased.

Joey went in first. "Wha-what happened?" he yelled.

"Let me see, move." Through the hole, I stood and couldn't believe the sight of our fort. Books were thrown everywhere, along with a pile of boxes that used to be our table. The empty plastic bottles we'd saved to recycle were scattered all about.

"Someone found our secret place, Kye! Look at it!"

"Yeah, but why'd they have to trash it?" I turned slowly around, taking it all in. "And who did it? No one comes around here; there are no houses for miles!"

"I don't like this. We better get out of here. What if someone is still around, watching us?"

I rubbed the hair standing up on my arms. I wouldn't dare let Joey see me scared. "Come on, you're being freaky. Probably just some prank. Are you sure you didn't tell anyone at school about this?" Joey looked up as I continued, "You did, didn't you? Now they had all summer to find it and scare the crap out of us. Good going, Joe!"

"Listen, Kye, I did not tell anyone, I swear. Why would I do that? I like this secret place. It's probably some serial killer!" He stood with eyes wide, ready to flee any second.

I'd had enough. I was scared, but a serial killer was going overboard. Just then, a show I had watched one night flashed through my mind. It told how serial killers hung out in parks and wooded areas. The way Mom had been lately, she might not even notice if I didn't come home. My heart sped, as I scanned the fort.

A rustling noise made me and Joey jump and spin around to see a lump under the plastic floor moving against the wall.

"Look!" I yelled to Joey, pointing at the ground.

"What the heck?" Joey groaned when he squatted down to get a closer look. Whatever it was scratched at a place where staples held the plastic to the wall, trying to dig under or get through somehow. It backed up enough to climb out over the plastic and made a run for it in the open. The intruder lunged for the secret door. With wide eyes, we watched the bushy striped tail, as the raccoon made its way to freedom.

"Some serial killer, JOE!" I glared at him. I held his gaze as long as I could until we both burst out laughing.

"Let's get this mess cleaned up. Here's some money. Here are some hotels. Remember, I was winning!" I said.

Joey rolled his eyes before he began stacking boxes to rebuild our game table. We picked up playing cards and empty bottles and tossed them into a corner. I held my stomach, as it flipped, when I thought someone had invaded my special place—my place to come and forget how everyday things were changing at home. It was Momma who helped me build my first fort from blankets, tables, and chairs when I was little. I remembered huddling under there with her at night, using a flashlight to make shadow animals on the blanket walls. We would giggle together when she tried to make them look like they were talking. But that was the old Momma. Knowing this place could change also made my gut wrench.

I invited Joey to ride home with me that afternoon for some milk and cookies. He rode his horse, Butch, next to me and Kiwi. Unlike my race to Joey's, we trotted the horses slowly back to my house. After all, I was in no hurry to get there.

Once home, Mom stood in the kitchen, still in her robe. When she saw us, she slipped out the side door into the dining room, barely speaking to Joey on her way out.

"Dang, who fired the maid?" Joey teased me.

I looked in the sink and remembered Mom had asked me to do the dishes. I scanned the rest of the kitchen and realized it would take more than clean dishes to fix this mess. "I guess it is kind of a wreck. Isn't it?"

"Not really, just compared to how your mom usually keeps it. She must be really sick."

"Must be." I got out the milk and cookies. While Joey ate, I picked up. He chatted with me as I washed the dishes. Then together, we dried them before he headed for home.

You got us pretty good today, God. That raccoon about made Joey wet himself. Hanging with him sort of cheered me up. Thanks, I needed that. I hate that Joey noticed the messy house. He's right; Mom must be sick. Or is she? Nothing makes sense anymore.

CHAPTER FIVE

Though storms aren't super common here in south central Montana, last night, lightning sparked the night sky and rumbling thunder surrounded the house. The wind whipped so strong that the tops of the tall pines swayed like dancers. We awoke to pine branches splintered on the ground and trees that looked like a plane had flown over, dipped down, and ripped their tops right off. Luckily, the storm spared the house, stable, and Dad's workshop in the shed.

Thank God, Momma'd been staying awake more lately. Once I was up, I couldn't wait to check on Kiwi. I babied her while Mom paid special attention to Sadie, our pregnant buckskin.

"She'll foal any day now." Mom felt under Sadie's rounded stomach. "Don't worry, Sadie. Your baby will be here soon. I know you're uncomfortable." She called to me, "It's been a while since we've had a new baby here. Are you excited?"

"So excited! Is she doing all right?" I remembered when Mom let me stay up late the night Kiwi was born. I was only seven, and most of it freaked me out. But I have such a good memory of watching her struggle to get her little, wobbly legs under her and finally stand up. Mom and I had hugged and cheered when Kiwi took her first shaky steps.

"She's calm and doing really well, considering how far along she is."

"Good. Kiwi seems okay, too. I need to go check on Dragonfly. I imagine the storm freaked him out. Poor guy."

Dad returned from pulling some branches off the lane.

"Dad, after I check on Dragonfly, can I call Joey?" I asked. "I wonder what their place looks like."

"Sure. Tell him we'll take a ride over there, here in a bit."

"You remember how Mrs. McLagan hates storms, Momma? I bet she'd like to see you. You'll come with us, won't you?" I asked.

"Okay, I'll go in and get dressed in a few." Mom headed to Josie's stall. She had trained Josie to be an expert trail horse. This horse could zip you up a steep hill so smooth like it was flat ground. But she got nervous trapped inside during a storm. "Calm down,

Baby. I know you'd rather be outside where you belong. Wouldn't you?"

Josie scattered the straw in her stall, shuffling in circles.

"Hey Kye, why don't you show me this new horse before we go?"

My brows raised in surprise before I led Mom to Dragonfly's stall. "He's a sad mess, Momma. Just watch what he does." I calmed my voice and called towards his stall. "Hey, Dragonfly. We're coming to see you." I stopped dead when Dragonfly popped his head over the stall gate and watched us carefully, as we walked toward him.

Mom walked slowly until she was nose-to-nose with the same horse that wouldn't even look at me. Softly, she said, "You're not going to be any problem. Are you, Dragonfly?"

I stood, hands outstretched. "How do you do that?"

Mom only winked at me over her shoulder.

Mom seems so much better today, please God, let her stay this way. While I watched her with Dragonfly, I thought how long it had been since we'd been for a ride together. If she could only stay like she is today, maybe together, we could tackle the trail we named Moses. Even though it's tough to ride, Mom and I loved riding it. It was long and winding with narrow paths zigzagging down a steep decline and then straight up the opposite hillside. Joey and I had named it Moses since it wound you around so much, you felt lost. It also took you through the water. Although, the water wouldn't part for you like God made it do for Moses and his people.

Joey's mom waved from the porch when we pulled up. "Hey, strangers! Takes a storm to get all three of ya to come see us anymore. Come on; have a glass of lemonade with me."

I saw Joey pulling a wagon with the four-wheeler around the yard. He stopped to pick up broken branches and twigs. "Thanks, but do you mind if I go help Joey?" I asked.

"Sure, sure, I'll save you a glass, Punkin."

I grinned over my shoulder, wondering when Mrs. McLagan would ever quit calling me Punkin. I overheard her ask my mom, "You feeling okay? I've never seen you look so puny."

To avoid Mom's excuses, I jogged toward Joey. He saw me coming, so he turned to meet me with his wagon. I walked past him, straight to the wagon and climbed inside, legs hanging over the edge. "Okay, let's go! Some storm, huh?"

Joey gunned the four-wheeler, heading for the next pile of branches to be collected. "No kidding!"

"Sounded like the house was going to take off for Oz or something. Looks like you got it worse." I pointed to our dads, already up on top of the shed roof, inspecting the damage from a large tree branch. "Your cattle okay?"

"Just skittish as all heck. Dad rode down to the bottom ground to check on them this morning. Hey, your mom came with you. She feeling better?" Joey asked.

"Seems to be, a little," I said, looking up at the porch where our moms sat, drinking lemonade, watching the men checking the roof. "Your mom survived the storm, huh? I know she hates them."

"Yep, she hid it pretty well this time."

We made a pass for some more sticks. When the wagon got too crowded, I scooted up behind Joey on the seat. "Hey, maybe the school blew down," I yelled in his ear as he took off to the burn pile.

"Yeah, that'd be great!"

After we unloaded the sticks and checked on the horses, we asked if we could take off for a trail ride. Agreeing on a short trail, I borrowed one of their four-wheelers, and we headed toward my house and on to Ruth Trail. The four-wheelers skidded back and forth in the mud, splattering clumps all over the back of our shirts and up into our hair. Joey raced to get around in front of me to spatter my face.

"I'm going to beat you!" He taunted when he got alongside of me.

"Oh no, you won't. Watch this." I flew past him, splashing through a huge puddle.

"You two be careful now. And don't be gone long." Mom hollered from the porch.

I was certain our laughing and teasing echoed back to the house.

We reached the well and dug into our pockets for coins to toss for our wish-making ritual. I was dying to ask Joey what he wished for but knew better. Long ago, we made a rule: "Don't tell wishes, or they might not come true." I pictured Momma sitting on the porch with Joey's mom, still not looking or acting quite like herself. I knew what I wished for.

Joey lowered the bucket and let it fill with water. "Geez, you need a bath."

"Think so?" I looked up, just as the water splashed right in my face. "Oh-my-gosh," the words spat out. Water poured off my hair and face. "That's it. You're SO dead!" I screamed at Joey. I reached for the bucket, but Joey was already on his four-wheeler, flying at top speed toward the house.

"You just wait, Joey McLagan. You'll get yours!" I yelled. I squeezed the water from my hair and wiped my face on my shirttail before firing up the four-wheeler to catch up with Joey.

Back at the shed, we played around having more water fights with the hose. We eventually got all the mud rinsed off the four-wheelers and mostly off ourselves. I was satisfied that I'd gotten my revenge by the time we finished. As we walked to the house, Joey said, "Hey, Mr. Riley's invited some of his rich investment friends to the rodeo this year. They're gonna donate some big money prizes on top of what

Riley already gives out! That's what Olivia told me anyway, so it could be wrong."

"Really? Cool. But wait. Olivia? When did you talk to her? Did she remind you that she beat me last year? I have got to find some time to work with Kiwi, so THAT doesn't happen again."

"She calls me sometimes. She's not so bad, Kye. Sometimes, I wonder if she's really as happy as she acts." He looked away from me, as he said it.

"What makes you wonder that?"

"I don't know. Something she said once made me think that her parents don't get along real well."

I tried to remember if I'd ever even seen her mom and dad together. "Yeah, I shouldn't talk about her. It's just that…Anyway, you think I can beat her this year, don't you?"

"Sure, you can. She just got lucky last year."

"Shut up, I can tell you're just saying that."

"Yep. I'm not stupid."

We laughed together and joined Mom and Dad.

"Looks like you two wet heads had fun," Mom said. Shaking her head, she smiled at Dad.

I threw the rags onto the back seat, said goodbye to the McLagans, and crawled into the truck to head home with my parents.

The next morning, something felt different when I entered the stable. I paused in the doorway and looked from stall to stall. The horses saw me, but they weren't shuffling to greet me as usual. I listened. Stillness filled the barn. Finally, I heard a sound. It took me a minute to recognize the suckling sound.

"Sadie!" I gasped, and then hurried to Sadie's stall. There, standing on wobbly legs beside Sadie, was the sweetest buckskin foal I had ever seen. "A boy," I whispered. "You had a beautiful boy." I watched for a while as the foal nursed his mother, batting his long eyelashes and flicking his stubby tail. Finally, I pried myself away. "It's a foal, Kiwi!" I squealed as I flew past on my way in to tell Mom and Dad the news.

CHAPTER SIX

The cool breeze brushed my face when I stepped out to the shaded porch where Dad leaned against the rail. "I see Mom was able to get Dragonfly out of the stall."

"Uh huh, that's about all though. Mr. Riley dropped off one of his horses last night. She's been working with it all morning." Dad smiled.

"Dang, I was wondering if she'd ever get back to her training. Now we can't keep her out of the stable. Weird." I walked up next to him and watched them in the training ring.

Dad nodded.

"She kept him in the ring for a long time yesterday, too. I asked her if she could take a break and time me and Kiwi running barrels, but she didn't want to stop working the horse." I pulled off my hat and pulled my hair back off my face. Turning the brim to the back, I pushed it back on my head. "But I wish she'd work with Dragonfly. He sure doesn't like it when I'm around."

Dad flipped my cap off my head. "Patience, kiddo."

"And since the foal was born, Mom's only spent the first few days with him. He's got tons of first weeks' training left to do."

"Have you worked with him?" Dad asked.

"A little, but I don't remember all that needs done when they're that young. Mostly, I've just been rubbing him down his neck and all around his face and mouth. I remembered that, to get him used to it for a bit someday. He still doesn't like it!" I watched Mom a little longer. "I'm gonna see if she'll go for a ride with me. That horse's had it."

"Good plan."

I ran out toward Mom. "Can you take a break and go for a ride with me on Moses Trail?"

"Hey, why not. We've not ridden that trail in quite a while."

We returned Mr. Riley's horse to the barn and saddled up Josie for Mom, Kiwi for me, and headed for the trail that began across the pasture. I was feeling pretty good when we rode past Dragonfly in the paddock. Surprisingly, he trotted to the fence and followed us for a little bit. I turned to watch him, waiting for him to duck and run. But he didn't!

About halfway through the pasture, Mom asked, "Wanna race?"

"You bet!"

"Yah!" We both yelled, and the horses began the race. Josie could skunk every horse we've owned in a race, so I wasn't surprised when Mom flew ahead. I was surprised at how hard Mom was kicking Jose's sides and smacking her neck with the reins. Josie could win without all of that business, and Mom knew it.

They reached the far hill way ahead of me, but Mom continued to push Josie. Usually, she gauged my speed and kept it a close race to keep me and Kiwi interested. Not today. Mom waited at the trail edge for us. Josie's nostrils flared with her heavy breathing. Her coat shone and was lathered with sweat.

"Boy, Mom, some run. I think racing her that fast wore her out before the trail."

"You're not being a sore loser, are you?"

Mom never snipped like that. "I'm not a sore loser. Just think you pushed her awfully hard. That's all," I answered.

Mom shot me a look from the tops of her eyes.

My saddle squeaked when I adjusted myself. I decided it would be wiser to keep quiet since I had really missed riding with her and training with her, too. I thought about how many of Mr. Riley's horses she'd let me help with—everything from two-year olds to cutting horses to prize-winning rodeo horses. When she had wanted to expand the ranch and take in rescue horses, we searched on the computer and gathered the details together. Mom had made me feel like I was such a big help with the idea. But then she just stopped talking about it, stopped riding with me, stopped everything.

Mom took the steeper ways up and down today, along the rocky edge. I felt Josie's nerves on edge, riding off the trail on uneven ground, but I decided to keep my mouth shut this time. Seeing the clearing ahead, I breathed a sigh of relief.

"Wanna race back?" she asked.

"No, you go ahead. We're just gonna take it slow and rest after that trail," I said.

"Suit yourself. Yah!"

Even though Josie was exhausted, she galloped away, hooves pounding the hillside. I leaned down and rubbed Kiwi's neck. "Poor Josie."

I was still confused or maybe upset about the race with Mom when I reached the paddock where Dragonfly waited at the fence. "Hey, Dragon—" Before I could get it out, he turned and ran away.

The screen door creaked when I came in looking for Dad. I found him in the kitchen writing invoices. "Dad, did you see Mom fly Josie across the pasture?"

"Yeah, she creamed you!" He grinned.

"Not that. Don't you think she's been acting kinda different again?"

Dad put his pen down and thought for a minute. "I don't know, Kye. I think she's just glad to be feeling better, trying to make up for lost time maybe." His blue eyes had a look that said different though, a worried look.

"Yeah, maybe."

I didn't know how to feel anymore. I was both happy that Mom was awake, but sad that she was awake and still so different.

I only planned to close my eyes for a few minutes on the couch before getting some training time in with Kiwi. But the next thing I knew, I woke up to the burning fumes of ammonia, stinging my eyes and nose. I sat up with a jerk. Why in the heck was Mom cleaning the window glass so hard, like she was mad at it?

"Hey, sleepyhead. I have a list of a few things I need some help with." She motioned with her rubber-glove-covered hand. "I stuck it to the refrigerator. It's not much. You should have time left today."

I snatched the list off the refrigerator and read over the few things, as I rolled my eyes. Half the stuff I'd been doing every night for weeks.

In the barn, after apologizing to Kiwi for us not getting to practice, I told her, "I don't get it, Kiwi. I thought I'd be able to do what I wanted today since Momma's actually doing things now. But she's changing by the week, and I can't keep up. Not with her changes or with all the stuff I have to do. Somehow, I'll make time, Kiwi. Even though sometimes I feel like I can't even stand up straight anymore, I'll make time."

After we talked, I went to see Sadie and her foal. I tried hard to remember the things Mom had taught me to do first with young foals. I moved gently toward the baby buckskin and slowly reached toward his side, keeping my eye on his sweet face. His hooves pattered the ground, and his muscles flinched. I rubbed his side until he seemed comfortable with that. Next, I rubbed down his legs like Mom taught me. He tried to shuffle away, so I stopped. But I didn't take my hand from him. After he calmed down, I removed my hand and rewarded him with some sweet talk and soft pats on his neck.

"That's a sweet baby. Next time, we'll try picking up that foot. See how ya like that." Momma should be doing this. I mean, I could do it, but she's the one with the training. He should have been worked steady from the first day he was born. I carefully placed a loose lasso around his neck, and then waited for him to settle. With my hand, I put pressure on his hindquarter, then gently dug my fingers in, until he moved a step. "Good boy, that's right." I told him as I rubbed his back. We did this again and again until he learned to move with the slightest pressure. "Look at you; you're so smart. Now let's work on the other side." We continued with his other hindquarter until he'd had enough for one session.

Later, after I finished Mom's list, I passed the kitchen and heard her still cleaning away. "Night, Momma."

Mom stopped mopping a minute. "Night, Sunshine. I'm going to finish these floors down here before I come up. See you in the morning."

Lord, I could have sworn that she had just mopped them yesterday.

CHAPTER SEVEN

My favorite part of summer had finally arrived. I'd get to work for cool Mr. Riley. When we headed down Shake Rag Road about six miles, we started seeing his stone fences. I guessed he owned over a hundred horses. Some of them he bred and sold for big bucks. Every year, he paid for his ranch crew to take a cruise. While they're gone, he hired kids to work at his ranch for two weeks. I bet he figured that kept us from getting bored over the summer and getting into trouble. And it gave us spending money. But this year was so different.

Come on, a sweatshirt, any sweatshirt. It's gonna be cold in the barn this early. I flung the clothes to the floor. I yanked open another drawer. "If I'd known Mom wasn't going to wake me up, like she said she would, I would have done this last night!" I grumbled under my breath and dug deep into my dresser drawer. "There it is!" Not only was I mad at Momma, I was also mad at myself. Even though I'd been so tired lately, that I couldn't wait for my head to hit my pillow, I still seemed to always lie there praying that I would stop worrying about what was wrong with my mom. "No way am I gonna make it to Mr. Riley's in thirty minutes. Takes fifteen to drive there."

"Kylie! Can you come down here and help me a minute?" Mom hollered.

"Hang on. I'm getting dressed." I pulled the sweatshirt over my head and rushed to the bathroom for my toothbrush. I squeezed on the toothpaste and tried brushing, while pulling on my boots.

"Kylie!"

Through a mouth full of toothpaste, I yelled, "I'm coming."

Mom stood in the pantry on a ladder. "Hand those boxes up to me, and I'll stack them on these shelves, out of the way."

"But Mom, we have to leave! Don't you have to get ready?"

"I'll be okay. Come on. Hand them up," Mom said.

I sighed. Then I reached the boxes up to my mom as quickly as she would take them.

"Okay, now there are three more over by the counter. Bring them, will you?"

"Mom, I can't be late. I have to get signed in. Can we do this later?"

"Kylie, bring me the boxes," Mom insisted.

I obeyed, then checked my watch when Mom finally climbed down from the ladder.

"Now, I'll just go up and change and brush my teeth, and then we'll go."

"You're just going to drop me off. You look fine. Can we just go?" I asked, starting to sound irritated.

"No. I'll be down in a minute," Mom said.

"Then never mind, I'm going to get Dad to take me," I said. "Thanks anyway." *For nothing*, I thought, as I grabbed my work gloves and slammed out the door.

Dad got me to Mr. Riley's ranch barely on time. Joey, in his usual good mood, made the mistake of teasing me for being almost late.

"Not funny, Joe," I snapped. "I tried to get here earlier."

As the morning passed, my mood improved. It helped when I found out we would be working in the Clydesdale barn. Surrounded by a whole stable full of these beautiful giants, I forgot about being irritated with Mom.

"Well, hello there, Miss Kylie!" Mr. Riley reached his hand out to greet me. "I'm glad to hear your mom has started on my new quarter horse. He's going to be a prize, that one. I can tell."

"Yes, she's been working with him quite a lot," I answered.

"I'm going to keep her busy this winter. I have several new horses this year. Most of them are pretty green."

"I'll tell her, Mr. Riley."

"I finished the flyers the other day for the Winter Rodeo. I'm excited about it. Proceeds go to the Billing's Children's Hospital this year," said Mr. Riley.

Behind Mr. Riley, I saw Olivia walking towards us, so I grabbed Joey's arm. "I can't wait. Well, we better get busy. See ya." I said, as I pulled Joey back to the Clydesdales away from Olivia.

Safely back with the Clydes, we shoveled stalls and spread straw. No grooming yet. First year kids went over safety rules for working around the horses. But Joey and I were on our third summer. Olivia was on a team in another barn, but she still managed to find me three times to ask how my training was going for the "big day." Maybe I would like her better if she had something—anything else—to talk about.

When lunchtime came, we joined the other kids in Mr. Riley's air-conditioned indoor arena. There were some tables and chairs set up to eat our sack lunches. Aside from eating, we spent lunchtime trading food, giggling over jokes, and complaining about summer being half gone.

"I barely had time to grab this yogurt," I said. I glanced over to Joey's lunch. He pulled from a huge bag: a peanut butter sandwich, a bologna sandwich, two kinds of chips, grapes, cookies, two pops, a pack of peanut butter crackers, and a fruit rollup. I looked at the other kid's lunches, then back at his lunch, then up to Joey. "Hungry?" I asked sarcastically.

The girl sitting across from him almost choked on her chips from laughing.

Looking at the tables covered with sack lunches, I remembered last year, when Mom had packed my lunch and made sure I arrived in plenty of time. This year, she never even woke me up.

By close to four o'clock, the muscles across my shoulders ached from lifting and stacking bales of straw. The other kids, who had waited in groups across the lawn, had slowly gotten picked up by their parents. It was only me, Joey, and Olivia left. Mom should have been here by now. I was enjoying resting for once, though, so I told Joey to go on without me when his dad pulled up.

Olivia came back from her mom's car, sounding way too excited. "I asked my mom if we could hang out for a little while until your mom gets here. She said that was good because she brought a book she wants to finish, anyway." Olivia plopped down right beside me.

As Joey got in his dad's truck, he glanced back my way. I made sure Olivia wasn't looking before I gave him a look that said, HELP!

After fifteen minutes of listening to Olivia listing all the reasons why my mom might have lost track of time, I got really irritated with Momma. I wanted to tell Olivia, "Believe me, I know more reasons than you could ever list!"

Another fifteen minutes passed with no sign of Momma.

Olivia's mom finally yelled from the car window, "Kylie, why don't you let us take you home?"

This was the first time that I wished I had a cell phone. But where we lived had horrible service anyway. I really didn't want Olivia's mom to take me home, but since Mr. Riley had left to get to a meeting, there was no way for me to use his house phone. And I couldn't ask Olivia's mom to wait in the car any longer. "Are sure you don't mind?" I asked.

"Not at all. Come on, girls."

Olivia looked so happy when she said, "Let's go, Kylie!"

I felt sick.

To calm my stomach and avoid Olivia's happy face, I melted into the seat, closed my eyes, and tried to calculate how many weeks I had to work with Kiwi before the rodeo. Finally, I heard the gravel on the tires and knew we had turned up my lane, so I opened my eyes. "What the heck?" Linens hung from makeshift clotheslines all over our front yard.

"What's going on?" Olivia asked.

"Summer cleaning, I guess." My eyes scanned the lines across the yard from all the way left of the house clear over to the yard on the right of the house. Every blanket, sheet, tablecloth, and rug we owned whipped in the wind.

"Looks more like you all got evicted!" Olivia said.

"Kye! Good, you're home!" Mom bounced down the porch steps and right up to Olivia's mom's car. "I've been waiting for you. I tried to sweep and mop in your room, but I can barely find your floor under all those clothes. Get up there and pick up that mess. Will you, Sunshine?"

"Um, Mom...Olivia and her mom brought me home when no one came for me," I said as I got out of the car.

"Oh, right. Thanks guys!" She leaned down to the window and gave a quick wave, before dismissing them. She turned back to me. "And grab one of those empty boxes at the bottom of the stairs. You need to go through and pull out all the clothes you don't wear anymore," she rambled on her way back to the house.

"But—" I stopped myself from saying more in front of Olivia and her mom. I thanked and said goodbye to them. They both looked confused, and then I hurried to catch Mom. "Wait! Why didn't you pick me up? Mr. Riley had to leave for a meeting, and everyone else left, except Olivia. I had to ride home with Olivia. Olivia, Mom! How embarrassing."

"Well, I thought your dad was picking you up."

"Well, he didn't." My voice shook when I said it.

"Come on, Kye, there's too much to do right now. I'm heading up to the resale tomorrow."

Realizing she was back to not caring about me, I knew not to bother arguing. Looking down at myself, filthy with dust and horsehair, I asked, "Can't I take a bath first? I'll clean my room later, before bed."

"No. You head on up there and get it done now. Thanks, hon!" Mom practically skipped past me to check the clothes hanging on the line. "I wish these would hurry and dry. I want you to help me hang out the others in the washer."

I rolled my eyes at Dad when he pulled up in his truck. When he got out, he spun a slow circle to check out the yard. "What are you girls up to?"

"Not sure what Mom's up to. I just got home."

"Really? I thought the shift was done at three," Dad said.

"It was. No one picked me up, so Olivia's mom had to give me a ride."

Dad's expression turned sharp, and he said to Mom, "This morning, I asked you to pick her up. I told you I had to run to the parts shop."

"She's here now. She's fine. And I need her to get up to her room and clean out her stuff and then help me hang out some more linens." Mom wiped the sweat from her face, while watching the sheets blow in the wind.

Dad looked at me with regret before he stepped closer to Mom. I didn't like the vibes I felt between the two of them, and I wanted to tell them it was okay; I would head upstairs and do what she wanted. But the look on Dad's face told me to stay right here.

"But you forgot her. What would have happened if Olivia had also gone home? This is not something you just blow off like you are doing. Come inside a minute. We need to talk," Dad said.

"I can't right now, hon. Look at all that needs done here." Mom waved her arms at the yard. "Kylie needs to get upstairs—"

"She's tired. She's upset. And I want you to come inside. Now." Dad opened the door and waited for Mom to finally come inside.

This is all my fault, God. I should have just done what she asked.

Over his shoulder, Dad said, "I'm sorry, Kylie. Why don't you go on upstairs, get cleaned up, and rest for a little while?"

I sat on the edge of my bed. Even with my door closed, I could hear my parents arguing downstairs. I held my stomach. After only a yogurt to eat all day, I should have been starved, but instead I just felt sick. When I couldn't stand it anymore, I grabbed some sweats and a t-shirt and crept out to the bathroom, hoping the sound of the shower would cover their loud voices.

My hair was still wrapped in a towel when there was a knock on my door.

"Hey, can I come in?' Dad asked.

"Sure." I sat up and turned down my music.

"You hungry, kiddo?" Dad asked, sitting down on the edge of the bed.

"Not really." I grabbed a book and flipped through the pages to avoid looking at him.

"Your mom's out taking down the things from the yard." He got up, went to the window and moved the curtain, so he could look out. "What'd you think when no one showed up to get you today? I'll bet you were worried."

I shrugged.

When I said nothing, Dad came back and picked up a book from my pile. He studied it a minute before going on. "I want you to know that won't happen again. I'll take you and pick you up the rest of the week, since your mom's so...distracted."

"Okay."

To change the mood, when Dad bent down to hug me, I said, "Anyone's gotta be better than Olivia."

The corners of Dad's mouth turned up, and he pulled the towel off my head. "You be nice to that girl. Even if she did beat you at the barrel race." Now he was laughing.

"I am nice to her! Even if she does remind me of that every time I see her. And always looks so...perfect. You should have seen what she wore today to shovel poop!"

"Well, who knows when Mom'll get finished. How 'bout a grilled cheese? I'm starving."

"Sure. Make one for Mom, too."

"I doubt she'll eat it, but I'll make it," he mumbled on his way out.

Hey, God. What a week. Between working at Riley's and keeping up with Momma, I'm bushed. I think she finally ran out of things to wash. But tomorrow, she'll probably have me start painting the barn or something. Ever since she forgot me, and they had that fight over it, Dad's been spending more time in the shop. At least I get to see him when he drives me to Riley's.

I rolled over on my back and yawned.

I miss my horses. Mom's been doing my stable chores and keeping me so busy inside, I've hardly talked to them at all this week. At least she's not sleeping all day anymore. That's good. Isn't it? But, God? I need time to work with Kiwi. I know it's still summer, and we've got time, but I have to win this year. Not just to beat Olivia; I mean, I really want to beat her. But Momma loves the rodeo so much. Maybe... well, you know. I could barely hold my eyes open. *Night, God.*

CHAPTER EIGHT

On the Fourth of July holiday, my family and Joey's would usually meet at the parade in town, and then later go to the fireworks together. This year, I pretended to be sick, so I could stay home and spend some time with the horses.

I watched from my bedroom window as my parents' truck left the lane. When they were out of sight, I changed my clothes and jogged to the stable. Tricking my parents put knots in my stomach, but it was the only way I would get to spend a whole day with the horses without Mom scheduling my every spare second. And besides, Kiwi must be feeling neglected. I stopped there first.

"There's my favorite horse!" I haltered Kiwi, before leading her out of the stable to the paddock where I dropped the lead and walked along, talking to my pal. Stopping to pick clover here and there, Kiwi heard my secret about pretending to be sick today, and lots of the other things on my mind. She followed behind, keeping her head almost on my shoulder. When she nosed my ear, I giggled. "Hey, that tickles!"

Follow the leader was a game we had played since I was young. I would run a little, stop, turn, and zigzag through the paddock, laughing as Kiwi followed me step by step. By the time we'd finished, I was feeling as close to my old self as I imagined possible these days. I decided to let Kiwi enjoy the sun while I went to check on Dragonfly.

Mom had cared for the horses before she left for the parade, so I only gave them a quick "hello" on my way to Dragonfly's stall. I walked slowly, prepared for whatever unwelcoming response he would have today. Usually, he'd either back up and look the other way or turn completely away from me, making it very clear he did not want me inside his space. Today, when I walked up, he was biting the air trying to catch this huge barn fly that must have been pestering him. I tried to stay quiet, but after the third chomp, again missing the fly, I couldn't stop from laughing. Dragonfly spun around. When he saw me, he began to back away, but stopped short. Then, he stared me straight in the eyes.

I froze. The smile also froze on my face. He studied me a long time before he took a slow step in my direction. His ears raised and turned toward me. Shocked, I slowly raised my hand, palm out. My heart raced when he brought his face close enough for me to touch him.

"Well, hello, Dragonfly," I said, trying to stay calm. "It is so nice to finally meet you." I stayed outside his stall, letting him get to know me. Finally, I took a chance and opened the door, taking only one step. Not wanting to push my luck, I waited in the doorway. When that didn't seem to bother him, I took a couple steps inside the stall. Dragonfly never took his eyes off me, and his look was soft and gentle. His muscles relaxed, and his tail rested without its normal anxious swishing or being tucked down in fear. If a heart could smile, that's what mine felt like it was doing.

I haltered him and led him out the door to the paddock with Kiwi. Curious what he'd do, I unhooked the lead and backed away. Dragonfly paused only a moment before he turned and trotted away, ears forward, head and tail held high. He didn't seem to even notice Kiwi while he circled me twice. And of course, Kiwi didn't mind the company. The third time, he stopped at my side, sniffed my shoulder, and dropped his head to graze.

"I'm not sure what changed, boy. But thank God it did. I was about to give up on you." I rubbed his neck. Dragonfly raised his head, and a breeze blew his forelock away from his forehead. "Well, look at that!" I traced my finger over the white marking across his forehead. It was shaped like wings. The thin white marking down his nose made the body. "A dragonfly!"

I searched for a soft piece of ground, sat down, leaned against a fence post, and enjoyed watching my friends, old and new. Now maybe I could figure out what kind of training this horse needed and start pushing Mom to help me. *Wish me luck, God.*

CHAPTER NINE

He trotted over to the fence where I stood. "Okay, Mr. Dragonfly, are you ready for some more exercises?" I was glad to see Dragonfly's ears perked up at the sound of my voice. "Hi!" I watched his eyes, they were soft. Not tight or wide open with white showing around them like when he first came here. His ears were forward and alert. "You're looking very happy today." I rubbed the side of his neck. "I finished my work as fast as I could. Momma left early this morning. She said she had to go to town again. Beats me what she does, but at least she's not sleeping." I held out my other hand and kept it closed. He sniffed at the grain I had hidden inside. "Good boy." I opened my hand and fed him the grain. "And at least she's not working herself...and me to death."

I attached the long lead to Dragonfly's harness, and we did some lunging exercises in the round pen. I'd been working on building his trust for the last week or so. Some days he was good, others not so good. "How about you follow me around the place today? Can I see how you do being led around?" I wrapped the lead like a lasso to shorten it, and we started our walk, keeping him near the barn, just in case he changed his mind.

He was doing great, so I was about to try walking him up and down the lane when I heard Mom in her truck returning from the store. "Hold on. I'll come help you carry stuff in," I hollered.

"That's okay, I got 'em. Thanks."

"Geez," I muttered, my stomach clenching at the sight of Mom's face when she turned toward me. I barely recognized her under tons of makeup. "That's what took her so long, another makeover. Those don't look like grocery bags. More makeup?" I asked Dragonfly.

I glanced around the yard. Things on the outside were getting back to normal after the big storm. The damaged tree branches had been trimmed and cleared. I sure wished things on the inside were back to normal.

"I wonder what Dad will think when he sees that?" I clicked my tongue for Dragonfly to follow me toward the stable. He tensed and backed up so quickly, I almost landed on my butt. "What are you doing? Come on." He stood frozen, which set my nerves more on edge than they already were after seeing Mom's new Broadway star look. "Dragonfly, let's go!" I tugged on his lead, but he held his ground. After a few more tries, I walked forward and reached for his harness. But as soon as I got in front of him, he spun around, startling me, and ran with his lead flopping, back toward the stable. He moved so fast I couldn't even grab the lead. I chased after him, only to find him with his nose in the corner of his stall, ears pinned back, and his rear end blocking me from coming any closer.

"Aww, Dragonfly. What happened? We were just having a nice walk. We're friends now. Remember?" I tried to worm my way into his stall to remove his harness. He nearly stepped on my foot twice and pulled his head away from me several times. "I am not getting my foot broken trying to get that off of you! Just keep it on." I wondered how we could have been having such a good day one minute, and then he took off running back to his corner the next? "You remind me of Momma!" I said over my shoulder on my way to Kiwi's stall.

Kiwi turned to me, happy to see me, as usual. Her creamy colored coat was dark with clumped dirt from rolling around earlier. "See, Kiwi. Didn't I tell you he had issues?"

Brushing the dirt off of Kiwi helped me calm down. Finally, I was back in the mood to do some training, so I got her saddled up and then led her out to the paddock for some circling. I stood still, passing the lead from hand to hand, as she ran circles around me. Keeping her close to me softened her ribs, so that when she raced, she'd come close to the barrels without knocking them over. After a while, I had her switch directions. "You're such a good girl, Kiwi," I said as I decided what to work on next. Luckily, we had plenty of drills to do. I was not in the mood to run the barrels while Momma just ignored us. The last time we ran them, Kiwi seemed to be picking up speed. I couldn't prove it, though, since there was no one around to time us.

I signaled Kiwi to stop and pulled myself into the saddle to race her to the fence. Just before we reached the fence, I turned her sharp, lifting her side with my leg, then sprinted her away from the fence. "Good job, girl." In about thirty yards, we made another sharp turn in the other direction, and we headed back toward the fence. We practiced quick stops and turns until my legs were shaky. Would this be enough to beat Olivia? Who knew? She probably wasn't doing everything by herself!

Afterwards, as I groomed Kiwi, I told her, "It's not only Dragonfly and Mom that are bothering me, Kiwi. Dad has to notice the weirdness around here." I worked her mane with the comb awhile, then leaned my head against Kiwi's jaw. "Maybe he doesn't notice. He's hardly ever up at the house anymore." I switched to the brush. "You'd think he'd notice the nights, though. I mean, when does Momma sleep? Last night, I woke up around one in the morning to the smell of fresh baked bread. The night before, the smell of chocolate brownies woke me up." I jerked my head up to look Kiwi in the eye. "But dinnertime! He must notice dinnertime. She marathon cooks like there are twenty of us. I think she can't decide what to make, so she makes everything." I rested my head against Kiwi again. "I like it out here with you."

CHAPTER TEN

Mom stood above my bed. "Kye, wake up. I have a great idea."

I opened my eyes to darkness. "What time is it?"

"Come on. If we leave now, we can catch the first shuttle bus to the city."

"Momma, it's dark! What are you talking about?"

"I know. By the time you get ready, the sun will be up."

"Ready for what?" I rubbed my eyes. The birds hadn't even started to sing.

"School shopping. You must need clothes, right? I haven't forgotten your thirteenth birthday is coming."

"What about the horses? I have chores."

"I already did the morning chores. Daddy will do the rest."

I looked out the window into the darkness, then covered my head with a blanket.

"Chop, chop, let's go," she said.

After I heard Mom leave my room, I flipped the blanket off my head. "Chop, chop? Oh well, why not?"

At the mall around one o'clock, we finally stopped for a quick lunch.

"My feet are killing me!" I complained. "I can hardly keep up with you! I think we've hit all three floors of the mall."

"I saw three more stores from the escalator. The clothes in their windows looked so cute. We'll find those next. I think I remember them being on the second level."

She acted annoyed with me when I told her that what she'd already bought was plenty to get me through the school year, plus summer. Gosh, you'd think she won the lottery or something. After lunch, we grabbed our bags and found the lockers. I was glad to be able to drop stuff in there because my hands were already sore from carrying so many bags.

We were barely out of the locker area when Momma said, "Oh, look at this salon. We should get our hair done!"

"Momma, really. The horses don't care what our hair looks like. Besides," I turned to Mom. "I like my curly mop. And now that you've decided to start combing yours once in a while, I like it, too." I put my arm around Mom's waist. She tensed, and I realized I had offended her. Luckily, the next store window caught her eye.

We stood in line at the coffee shop. I watched Mom's eyes dart from menu to menu, trying to decide on her coffee. "I'll have my usual, caramel machi whatever it's called," I said.

"Okay, when it's our turn, you go right ahead and ask for that." Mom laughed, as she still struggled with what she wanted.

I wanted to ask her so many things about the way she was acting, but instead, as we walked away with our coffees, I just said, "I miss you, Momma."

She looked surprised. "Why? I haven't been anywhere."

I sipped my coffee. "I know, but you've been really busy. Thank you for taking me shopping with you today."

Mom shifted her bags to one hand and put her arm around my shoulder to squeeze me to her side. "It's been a fun day. Now we just need to remember where those lockers are, so we can get the rest of our things."

While we waited for the last shuttle home, I rubbed my stomach expecting it to explode. "I am so stuffed! I loved that chocolate shop. And the cinnamon pretzels stand. And the cookie store. Ugh! It sure feels good to sit." I took a deep breath, then gazed at the pile between us. "Man, look at all these packages." I looked away when I started feeling uneasy. I'd never seen Mom swipe her credit card like she did today without even checking prices. It reminded me of the time Joey and I went into the arcade at the pizza parlor. The pinball machine we played must have been stuck. Pop, pop, pop, the free games kept adding on and on. I remembered feeling the excitement, followed by that twist in my gut that made me wonder if we should stop playing and tell someone the machine was broke. That was exactly like the twist in my gut right now, every time I looked at the pile of packages.

Dad turned down the news when I dragged in the house behind Momma. "Hey, how was the trip?"

"It was fun. Dad, look at all the clothes Momma bought for me. I guess I got an early birthday this year."

My dad's smile faded, as he watched Momma bring even more bags in from the porch. They locked eyes, and I swore the look on his face was like he wanted to ask, "What in the world?" Which was just what I had been wondering all day.

I pretended not to see his expression. "Thanks again, Momma. That was fun." I kissed her cheek. "I'm beat. Night."

"Okay, I'll be up early tomorrow to try to catch up on all the new jobs that've been coming in." Dad yawned. "So now that I know you're home safe, I'm turning in, too."

Momma gave him a quick hug before he headed upstairs.

"Kylie, wait. Don't go to bed yet. I want to see your new clothes."

Wondering how she seemed to have even more energy now than when we left, I said, "You saw already. I tried them on at the store."

"Yes, but not together in outfits. Come on, it'll be fun. Here put this one on first. Look how this stripe in the sweater matches the shirt." Mom fussed with each outfit. "Okay, now walk down to the doorway and back, so I can see you."

I felt silly, like I was modeling on a runway, but I was too tired to argue. Mom's mood had turned weird, agitated or something, so I tried on the outfits as quickly as possible, so I could go to bed.

The next morning, I called Joey early. "Hey. I know you're not into girl-clothes or anything. But you gotta come over and see the clothes my mom bought me yesterday."

"Yeah, early birthday and school clothes."

"Good! See ya."

I took a quick shower. Afterwards, I laid the clothes out all over the living room, matched into outfits. On the way into the kitchen to mix some grape drink for Joey, I ran right into Mom coming out with her hot coffee.

"Sorry, Momma! You okay? Don't worry. I'll get it." I rushed to get towels and brought them back to wipe the floor.

"Kylie!"

Mom's yell made me jump. Then I saw the new clothes—thrown everywhere.

"Where did you get these?" Mom shouted. "Don't tell me. You steal things!"

Mom grabbed my shirt and pointed a finger in my face. "You are taking this all back!" she growled, then she turned and bolted up the stairs. "Little thief!"

"Momma?" My voice cracked, and I was too shocked to say more.

Finally, when able to turn, I saw Joey peering through the screen door. For a change, his hair was away from his eye, and he looked like he had just seen someone purposely run over a fawn. I opened my mouth, willing words to come out, that would cover up for what we both had just seen happen.

There were no words.

Nothing.

"I-I'll come back, Kye. I'll come back another time," Joey said finally.

I watched him ride away. As soon as he was out of sight, I fell onto the couch and curled into a ball. What the heck was that all about? Why did Momma do that? *Don't cry. I won't cry.*

I sat up, took a deep breath for strength, and ran upstairs. "Momma!" I called to the closed bedroom door. "I did not steal those clothes! Don't you remember? We went shopping. You bought them for me. I am not a thief!" I waited, but she didn't respond. "What's wrong with you, Momma? You are scaring me."

Finally, I heard Mom crying. "Nothing, Kylie. Nothing is wrong with me. I just, I have to think about this. Leave me alone, okay?"

I worked in the stable harder than ever, cleaning stalls, polishing saddles, and brushing horses that didn't need brushing. I walked down to Dragonfly's stall. When he saw me, he spun away so fast, he bumped his head on his feed pail. With my head dropped, I returned to the door to watch for my dad to come home from town. Should I tell Dad? Will Momma tell him I stole?

Finally, Dad pulled up. When I reached the truck, the words burst out, "I didn't steal the clothes, Daddy!"

"What? What's the matter, Kye?" Dad asked. He climbed out and leaned against the truck.

"I didn't even ask for the clothes. I didn't pick them; Momma did! She said it was for my birthday. Now they're all over the floor, and she doesn't remember that she bought them. She called me a thief!" I shook from holding back the tears. "You saw them last night. Right, Daddy? I never stole anything!"

Dad held me until I calmed down. "It's okay. I believe you. Maybe she wore herself out and got herself in a slump again. You know, sometimes that

Irish temper comes on, and she says things she doesn't mean." Dad knelt to look me in the eye. "You wait out here a little while. Okay? I'll go talk to her. But don't worry; it's gonna be alright."

I had already done everything I could in the barn, so I walked to the pasture wondering what Mom was telling him. With the windows open, once in a while, I heard their voices creep outside—sharp voices, loud voices.

I couldn't stand it anymore. I was heading inside to beg them to stop arguing, but Dad met me at the door. "Mom's gonna stay in her room today."

"Daddy?"

"Don't worry, honey. She's confused; that's all." He held the door, and I came inside.

Slowly, Dad started to pack up all the clothes. I told him I didn't want any of it, but he insisted I keep the turquoise shirt, with mother of pearl snaps, that we picked for me to wear to the rodeo and a few jeans for school.

"I never want to see that other stuff again. Will you take it back for me, Dad?"

Dad nodded and then grabbed the bags that I didn't want and took them outside. I watched out the window as he put them behind the seat of his truck.

God, maybe Daddy remembers Momma's Irish temper, but I've never seen her act this way. I pray to never see it again. The look on her face, when she had me by my shirt, flashed through my mind. *What's wrong with her, God? What is wrong? I don't even know her anymore.*

CHAPTER ELEVEN

A week passed, and whatever had made Mom so sleepy had returned. The stealing had not been brought up again. That was just fine with me.

I'd avoided Joey long enough. "Hey, what's up?" I asked when he answered my phone call.

"I've been trying to call you all week. Wondered if you'd ever call back," said Joey.

"I'll ride my bike down if you'll wait at your lane for me. We could hang out." For the first time, since Mom's explosion, the idea of hanging out with Joey felt comfortable. But I was not ready yet to invite him to our house. Who knew if Mom would be shuffling around the house in the clothes that she'd slept in or she might be all dolled up, ready to go on a shopping binge? Either way, she had shown no interest in me or the horses since our shopping trip.

The long ride felt good. I pedaled fast. But I was late and sure that Joey would complain when I rode up. My untied hair blew about in the wind. I skidded to a stop in front of Joey and tried to mash my curls back into some kind of order. Joey had a dirty, red ball cap pulled down to shade the late summer Montana sun from his face.

"About time," he said.

I rolled my eyes and dropped my bike, then plopped on the ground to catch my breath. "Ouch!" I squealed and leaned to dig in the dirt under my rump. I held up a jagged rock. "That ought to bruise the ol' bootie."

"I'd bruise your ol' bootie if you'd left me here in this sun waiting on you one more minute," Joey said, trying to sound mad. Slowly though, the corners of his mouth turned up into a grin.

I dusted myself off and gave him a smirk that said, "'You know you can't be mad at me.'"

"Wanna ride the horses across the pasture?" he asked.

"Let's go!" My face lit up. "Can I ride Butch?" The creamy Appaloosa, my favorite of the McLagan's horses, had the sweetest personality.

"Now, why am I not surprised that you'd ask for the fastest horse we got? Come on. He's all saddled up and waiting for you," Joey said.

We rode our bikes up the lane toward the stable.

"You know, I would have called sooner if I'd known I'd get to kick your butt in a race…again," I teased.

"Yeah, yeah, we'll see about that."

While racing Joey, breathing fresh air, and feeling the hot sun tanning my shoulders, I didn't feel so dead inside. I didn't even have to force a fake smile after barely reaching the edge of the pasture before Joey. I think it was a real one.

"Oh, quit your pouting, Joe. You knew I'd win."

"Yeah, whatever." Even if Joey had ridden Butch, he probably would have let me win, but he managed to act annoyed. Changing the subject, he asked, "How's Sadie's foal doing? Have you started working with him?"

"I have some, but he needs more. I wish Mom would—I mean, I worked with him last week trying to desensitize him. I put some balloons in his stall and walked through them, so they moved all around. And I turned a chair upside down to watch what he would do about that. He's still pretty shy of most things."

"I hope you didn't spook him too bad."

"Oh no, I didn't do it all at once. He's so darn sweet; I'd never do that to him! And Sadie was in the stall with him."

We continued to chat like old times, neither one of us bringing up Mom and what happened in the living room that day.

That afternoon, I stepped from our sunny yard back into a house of gloom. Blinds closed tightly; drapes pulled together. The sunshine, and the good feelings that came with it, had been blocked from our house while Momma slept. My heart hurt. Was it too much to wish for just one full day where my heart felt happy?

CHAPTER TWELVE

All week, I rushed through the chores, including the house chores. Mom was letting the place fall apart again. Working fast gave me more time to run drills with Kiwi. Just a little faster time, and we would be able to win this year. We had to win. By now, I didn't even want Mom's help. I just wanted to win. I wanted her to see us win. I wanted her to know that I did it all alone! I did all the training: without her help, without her even noticing, and without her even coming outside!

Dad must've been working down by the burn pile. The scent of burning brush drifted past, as I circled Kiwi in the round pen until I was dizzy. We switched to flexing her head side to side. "Yeah, I know you know this, Kiwi. Come on, nose to my boot. Yep, now, nose to my other boot. Good girl!" She responded to me at the gentlest touch. It felt good to spend so much time with her. When we finished, I leaned over and rubbed Kiwi's neck while we cooled down with a pasture walk. "I know I worked you hard today. These drills will make you stronger and faster. Maybe if we time well, that'll get Mom to like me again. Or at least maybe she'll like you." When I looked up toward the house, I felt a tiny pinch in my heart. There was no sign of Mom.

I'd spent more time awake than asleep during the nights. I hadn't found a way to turn off all the junk racing through my head every time I closed my eyes. And the only way I could get everything done was to get up super early. On my way to ride Kiwi the next day, I wondered how long a girl could go with only a few hours of sleep. My arms felt weak when I hoisted the saddle onto her. I rested for a minute, and then wiped the sweat from my brow. "No time for feeling tired. Got things to do. Don't we, Kiwi?" I hurried and buckled the strap, mounted Kiwi, and rode out.

When Joey showed up on his four-wheeler, I tensed in the saddle. As much as I used to pray for my mom to come outside, I didn't want it today. Not after what Joey saw the last time he was here. Kiwi and I rounded the second barrel. Please, Momma. Just stay inside and sleep like you've been doing. No more scenes in front of Joey.

Kiwi shot across the pasture. She skid on her approach to round the first barrel. She leaned in for her turn. The saddle slipped to the side. I tried to shift my weight to stop it, but it was too late. It swiveled around, flinging me toward the ground. I reached out, trying to break the fall.

I heard a voice in the distance, like a slow-motion echo. "Ooohhh!"

My eyes cleared enough to make out Joey's blurred face.

"Don't move, Kye! You're okay. Just sit still a minute. You're alright, okay? Don't move!" Joey stammered, kneeling beside me.

I looked up at Joey, my pain hurt worse than any pain I'd ever felt. "I'm…not…going…anywhere, Joe."

Joey ran for help.

My head throbbed so bad that the sky started to spin. Finally, Joey got back with Dad.

"I'm right here, kiddo. Lay still." Dad took my hand. "Joe, call 911. Get Mom."

Joey leapt onto the four-wheeler and sped to the house.

Why did everything look so strange? "What happened? Where's Momma?"

CHAPTER THIRTEEN

That evening after finally getting back from the ER, Joey called. I listened to him describing to me how I flung off Kiwi. He said that I hit the ground so hard that he thought it shook. He blabbered on about how it was a good thing he got there when he did. I'd never heard him talk so much. I guessed I had scared him. "I'm okay, Joey. I promise."

I gently touched the lump on my head. "They said I have a concussion. I just have to rest a couple of days, until my headaches go away, and I get my balance back." I remembered how tired I was when I saddled up Kiwi, and I remembered my saddle slipping sideways. I always double cinch the saddle. I knew what could happen if you didn't since I was a little kid. It could have been worse than just a concussion.

How could I have forgotten to do that? Then I thought about how Momma had gone back to bed as soon as we got home, and I started worrying about who was going to feed the horses tonight. My head always spun with worry.

That's why I forgot.

CHAPTER FOURTEEN

A week later, a rich brown quarter horse circled Mom in the round pen. I loved days like this. The yard, the pasture, and the trees were covered in different shades of green. The sky seemed bluer somehow, and it took away part of the gloom I'd been feeling. Plus, Momma was feeling better.

"Mr. Riley's right. That's one smart horse," I yelled from the fence.

"Gorgeous, too. I love him!" Mom stopped training and led Cinnamon Charlie, Mr. Riley's new gelding, to me. "Look at his coat. It's such an unusual brown."

I reached to rub his side. "Like hot chocolate."

"How's your head today?" Mom asked.

"Better. I'm still kind of weak, but I'm not as dizzy. I wish I could ride. We're going to have so much catching up to do if we want to be ready for the rodeo."

"You have time, Kylie. It's not until winter. Feeling strong enough to lead Kiwi around the barrels a couple of times?"

I cocked an eyebrow at Mom, shocked that she was interested. I hustled to the stable before she changed her mind. Since the ground was uneven, I had to work on keeping myself steady. Kiwi and I finally made it to the pasture where the barrels were set up. A damp grass smell lingered in the air from yesterday's rain. Dad came up from the shed, and then stopped to watch. After Mom tied Cinnamon Charlie, she walked beside me.

"Start here. Just like you're going to race her," Mom said. "We'll walk over and around the first barrel."

Kiwi circled the barrel, shoulder close but not touching.

"Good girl!" Mom said to Kiwi. "Talk to her as you walk to the next barrel," Mom told me.

I noticed Mom drop back to watch Kiwi, as we neared the next barrel.

"That's right, Kiwi. We round this one and head for the next," I said.

Close to the third barrel, Kiwi slowed her walk. I cut close to the barrel, as she rounded it, but Kiwi swung wide.

"That's what I thought she'd do," Mom hollered to Dad.

"Kylie. Stop there, next to the barrel. Good. Now, get her up next to you and talk to her," Mom said.

"See, girl. It's okay. This barrel's okay."

"She's not worried about the barrel. She's worried about you. She remembers you getting hurt at this spot," Mom said.

I looked up at Dad, who now stood next to us rubbing Kiwi's side. "I think I'll start walking barrels with her every day. It'll be good for both of us," I said.

Mom and I took the horses back to the stable. A loud whinny coming from the end of the stable made me jump.

"Who was that?" Mom asked.

"That's Dragonfly. Never heard him do that before."

I looked down toward Dragonfly, and he leaned his neck farther over his gate to see us better with gentleness in his eyes. "So, you're having a good day today?" I asked the horse. "Okay, we'll come see you if you want."

Dragonfly tossed his head and whinnied again, even louder than before.

"Was that a yes?" I asked.

When I got to the stall, he slowly brought his head close and nuzzled my cheek.

"Amazing. I can't believe the change in him lately," I told Mom.

"Mr. Jinks called about him the other day. He told me he bought Dragonfly at auction when he found out that he had been re-homed several times before. People just keep giving up on him because he's so unpredictable. He thought he may be Dragonfly's last chance."

"Aww, poor Dragonfly." I cupped his muzzle in my hands and kissed his nose. I thought back to Dragonfly's moods. "You're just sensitive. Right, buddy?" A sensitive horse. I remembered reading something about this somewhere.

I looked over my shoulder and met Mom's eyes. *Thank you, God. Mom's eyes aren't dull today.*

CHAPTER FIFTEEN

I had to wake Momma this morning, so we wouldn't be late for my doctor's appointment. Now, while waiting for the doctor, she sat in the chair, yawning. I noticed the spark had gone again from her eyes. "Tired, Momma?"

"Uh-huh. Pretty tired, Sunshine."

Doc Jordan's office smelled old and sterile at the same time. I'd heard my parents talk about how it had been a drugstore thirty years ago. When the store outgrew the corner of the old, or as Dad called it "nostalgic," downtown building, they said Doc was happy to find the space with a suite above, where he and his wife could live. Mom always loved the way the office was decorated with antiques that wouldn't fit upstairs. She thought Mrs. Jordan collected beautiful things. Once when Mom praised the furniture, Mrs. Jordan said, "Just because you're at the doctor's office doesn't mean you can't be warm and cozy."

Finally, Doc called us into the room. "Have a seat."

I climbed up on the table he motioned toward, then sat on the edge.

"So, Kylie, I hear you want to ride those horses of yours."

"I'm ready, Doc. I'll be careful. I'm fine now. Really."

Doc smiled, nodded, and reached for a folder on his desk. After checking me over and asking a bunch of questions, he said, "If you promise not to fall on your noggin again, you are clear to ride."

"Thank you, Doc!" I wanted to hug him.

His eyebrows rose when he looked at Mom sitting slouched in her chair, staring out the window. "You feel okay?" He moved over and felt Mom's forehead and startled her.

She scooted up straight in her chair. "Yes. I'm fine."

"Isn't that great, Momma? I'm cleared to ride! Can I ride when we get home?"

"We'll see." She frowned at me, then went on. "I don't want you getting hurt again. We'll see when we get home."

This was not the response I expected. Just last week, she was excited about this doctor's appointment and my chance to ride again.

"You've seen for yourself how dangerous horseback riding can be. I don't want you getting hurt again," Momma snapped.

"Momma!"

I looked at Doc for support, but he only changed the subject. He said to call him if I experienced any more dizziness.

I smiled at Doc, but thoughts raged inside my head when I looked at Mom. *Oh, Momma, what's wrong with you?* I pressed my mouth closed to keep those thoughts from coming out. I didn't dare look back at Doc because I was so mad and embarrassed, I was sure to cry.

At home, I got out of the truck, making sure to head the opposite way that Mom headed. I flung open the doors to the stable, and the familiar smell of sweet oats, old wood, and manure greeted me. The grey, weathered barn wood and dirt floors comforted me.

I looked in on Sadie Faith and her foal. They made a beautiful pair, Sadie with her creamy, burnt sugar coat and white mane. She looked at me from her dark eyes, then leaned her neck down to nudge her foal, lying in the straw beside her. I couldn't believe how much he had grown. Montana Sky, that's what I would name him. It would be a perfect name. He had light buckskin markings, dark gangly legs, dark mane, and matching stubby tail. He looked up at his momma through sleepy eyes.

I moved over one stall to the proud father. The sign overhead read, "Tucker Tenacious," and it fit him exactly. I remembered when Mom trained Tucker. "This horse is stubborn." she had said. But when he finally gave in, he soaked up his training like a sponge.

Mom says now, "There is no end to what this horse can learn."

"Proud daddy, you're a good boy, aren't ya, Tucker?"

The next stall over belonged to Slugger Sam. Slugger's all white face, except for the brown patch around his right eye, gave him his name. The rest of him was mostly brown with white splotches here and there. His looks matched his personality. Slugger Sam was a hard-working horse, but one that only an experienced rider could enjoy. Not at all like his neighbor, Handsome Hans, the beautiful, sorrel red horse with white from between his eyes down to his nostrils. Hans was a sweet, gentle-natured horse. My mind wandered as I stepped into Hans's stall. *Come on, Momma! You would have let me ride last week. Why'd you have to go and flip again? Especially now that Doc said I could ride!*

CHAPTER SIXTEEN

When school started in early September, I boarded the bus for a long, boring ride. I pulled a book from my backpack to pass the time, but by the fifth bump, I gave up. Sometimes, Joey brought his game player. Not often, though, since I embarrassed him by winning every single game we played. I still hadn't told him I had my own player and that same game at home to practice. Usually, I loved teasing Joey because he'd get that shocked look on his face when I scored a higher level than he did. But not today. As we got closer to town, we picked up more kids. The bus filled with the sounds of boys trying to sound tough and girls talking and giggling. I closed my eyes and tried to tune them out.

"What's wrong? You still asleep?" Joey asked me.

"I'm awake . . . barely."

"We're almost there. You better come alive."

The bell clanged overhead when we walked

through the doors to Smithson Junior High. The musty smell was familiar but not welcoming. I found my home room and took a seat while the others complained about the heat and opened more windows. Every time someone asked me how my summer was, I'd lie. "Great!" Except for my concussion, a new horse that hates me most of the time, and my Mom turning into some mood-shifting stranger!

The teacher, Mr. Jackson, passed out the schedules and locker assignments. We were released from class early so we could find our lockers and have time to practice our combinations.

I made my way through the crowds of kids, dodging the ones not paying attention while they searched for their number on a locker. My chest tightened, and my stomach did flipflops. I reached locker 114 and pulled out the combination. Right 21, left 3, right 12. I jerked up the handle. Nothing happened. I started over. Right 21, left . . . Crap, I passed three twice! Right 21, left 3, right 12. Again, I jerked the handle. Nothing. I jerked again. My chest clenched tighter. Now I had a painful knot in my stomach. I kicked the bottom of the locker. Just then, a hand laid on my shoulder.

"Easy, buddy."

I flew around, not in the mood for razzing, to see Joey's one-eyed grin. I tried to calm down and handed him my combination. "Open the stupid thing, will ya?"

Joey popped the locker open on the first try.

"Hiiiiiiii   Ky-leeeeee!" I heard the high-pitched greeting from down the hall, then suddenly wished I could fit into my locker and close the door. I turned, with a forced smile, to greet Olivia. She quickly turned her attention to Joey.

Joey fidgeted in his backpack and pulled out his schedule. "I gotta go find my next class. See ya," he blurted out and vanished.

For some reason, I just did not like Olivia. Maybe because her long hair always looked so silky smooth. Last year, she wore it in a zillion different hairstyles. Or maybe, because Olivia never ran out of new, perfectly-matching-down-to-the-socks   clothes. I looked her up and down and realized I had never known a girl who was such a...girl.

"Oh, look. My locker's right next to yours!" Olivia said in that shrill, girlie voice that made the back of my neck tickle in a bad way.

"Yeah, look at that." I slammed my locker shut with my hip. It clanged much louder than I expected. I could feel her eyes on me, so I practically ran to my next class—anything to escape talking with her.

At the end of the day, I looked at my schedule. On top of everything going on at home, I'd had my least favorite teacher for two classes, Olivia in three classes, and Joey in zero. I decided to hate school this year.

CHAPTER SEVENTEEN

The bus dropped me off at the end of the lane after school. I passed Dad in the shop working on a trailer. *Don't bother coming in before dark.* I wanted to tell him. *You never do any more.*

Inside the house, I found Mom sleeping again. I opened my backpack, pulled out the first week's assignments, tossed them on my bed, and then headed outside to begin chores.

Dragonfly had gone back to disliking me. It really bothered me that Mr. Jinks, his owner, expected him to be trained by now. I went to Drangonfly's stall and got the usual "spin and ignore" from him. "WHY do you HATE me?" I yelled.

Dragonfly flinched, and my heart did the same.

"Did I scare you? I didn't mean to scare you. I like you." I opened the stall door, and he shuffled to the side I went toward, blocking me. "There's not much time left for all the training you still need. Mom's not doing it anymore, so that leaves me. I really thought that you would be able to help get her back to her old self. I guess I was stupid to think it would be that simple." I slapped his hind end lightly, trying to get him to turn, with no luck. "Okay, but I'll be back. You can have your way today, but I'm not giving up on you." Rubbing my sleepy eyes, I left him alone.

Why does he have to be so sensitive? The thought reminded me to find an article I had read. Back in my room, I flipped through a few of my horse magazines until I found it. As I read, I thought about Dragonfly, now knowing exactly what to do.

I headed back out to the barn. But this time, I stopped outside and tried to think of happy thoughts. The way I'd felt lately, that was not easy to do. I breathed slowly in and then out a few times, while I searched my memories. The year that Dad surprised us at Christmas time, when I was eight or nine, came to my mind. We had tons of snow that year. He told me and Mom to bundle up as warm as possible and then meet him behind the barn. When we got there, he had rented a sleigh, bells and all! It was led by Mr. Riley's Clydesdales. We all snuggled under the blankets in the sleigh and took a long ride until we finally started getting too cold. I think we had even sung carols. I remember telling my parents that I would never forget that day!

Once I caught the feelings in my heart that I'd had that day, I eased into the barn. "Hey, Dragonfly. I'm back. I have a story to tell you. Are you in there?"

Slowly, he turned and came closer to his stall gate.

"How do you feel about Clydesdales? They are huge, aren't they?"

He looked at me curiously. I slowly reached to pet his jaw. Soon, I had him harnessed and out of the stall. By the end of the story, we had walked together up and down the lane and all around the paddock, stopping here and there to just hang out together.

Afternoons after school all seemed the same: Mom in bed, Dad working, me trying to cook, clean, wash, train the foal, win over Dragonfly, and care for the other horses. Everything but what I wanted to be doing, barrel drills on Kiwi. And since Mom was a horse trainer--or at least used to be--learning about how to help Dragonfly from an article really bugged me.

Saturday morning, I scooped scrambled eggs from the sizzling skillet onto a plate. I tipped my head to look into the living room. The emptiness made me lose my appetite, like every other time I tried to eat. I scraped the eggs into the garbage and headed outside.

Watching Sadie's playful foal cheered me up. He'd step away from Sadie and skitter in a circle, head bobbing like, look at me! Then he'd hurry back next to his mom, where he was safe for a minute, before trying his independence again. I tethered Sadie to one side of the stall, so I could work with the foal's feet. I started at the front leg and rubbed him down to the hoof. When he calmed, I lifted his foot and patted the bottom of his hoof. "Good boy, nice job lifting that foot for me." I pretended Dad watched me train the foal. By the fourth foot, Sadie was getting impatient, and the foal sensed it. "Okay, one more pat and we're done." I placed his foot down and praised him more, before untying Sadie. I wished Mom would decide if she's selling him or keeping him, so I could officially name him, Montana Sky.

I imagined Dad asking me about his progress.

"His training's really simple for now. Just gets him to trust us. We'll keep adding things, though. Soon, he'll know how to lead and yield and all that. He's real smart."

"You've inherited your mother's horse abilities; you sure didn't get them from me," Dad would say.

But of course, Dad's not here. Nobody's here.

Sunday evening, I plopped onto my bed, rolled over onto my elbows with my hand supporting my chin. There, on the nightstand, was my unfinished homework. "Ah, crap." I reached out for it, my cheek touched the bed, my eyes rolled back, and that was all I remembered.

CHAPTER EIGHTEEN

In the bathroom mirror at school, under the fluorescent lights, my eyes looked more shadowed than ever before. My cheeks used to be round and rosy; now they looked pale and sunk in. My wrinkled T-shirt hung untucked, and my jeans bagged off my butt and thighs. "Real nice," I told that girl in the mirror. After I pulled my hair into a ponytail, I rushed out the door to get to class before the bell rang.

"Hey, wait up!" Joey shouted. "I'll walk with you." He caught up and held up a piece of paper. "I'm going to the office to make some copies."

"Sure." Cologne reeked in the air when he got close. I leaned over and sniffed him. "Eew. What's that smell?"

"What? Nothing!" Joey's eyes watched Olivia swing past. "I can't believe it's already midterms. You got tests today?"

"Yeah...probably."

"Probably? What do ya mean, probably? You're the study freak." Joey looked me up and down, brows together. "I heard this history midterm is gonna be really hard."

"Oh? Can't wait," I said. *Joey, I don't give a crap.*

Joey tilted his head, so the hair fell away from his eyes. "You okay?"

"Yeah. Here's my room. See ya later." I ducked into a classroom.

I made it through the first half of the day, faking my way through the midterm exams. History class was after lunch. Joey was right; the history test was two pages long. Since I hadn't read any of the material, and I'd been too worn out to think about schoolwork, I randomly picked my answers. True-False-True-False. Circle A-circle B-circle C the next time.

After everyone finished the test, we could talk until the bell rang. One of the boys who sat behind me tried to impress Olivia. I heard him digging around in his backpack when he kicked the leg of my chair then bumped his desk into the back of me. If I put my head down on my desk, maybe I could block him out before I turned around and said something else creepy. The desk smelled like old wood and erasers. He stopped kicking, but he began blabbing to Olivia.

"Hey, did you see the lunch lady today?" he asked her.

"Which one?"

"The one that acts like she's crazy. She's nuts, man. One day, she comes to our table and starts talkin' about nothin'. She went on and on, talkin' real fast. Weird." His foot thumped against my chair, and I jumped.

"She's not so bad," Olivia whispered.

"Then the next day, she'll be all quiet and barely look at us," the boy continued.

Olivia told him to stop being mean, so he turned to the boy next to him and asked him the same question.

I kept my head down on my desk. My knee bounced up and down, up and down, as I listened. I caught myself twirling my hair around my finger.

He continued, "Yesterday, I walked past here after lunch. This big crash comes from the kitchen. Someone starts yellin'. It was her. She was loud! You'd of thought the place was empty, the things she was sayin'. She come flyin' outa the kitchen and saw me, then she just stopped and stared. She's a kook!"

I tried to picture this person they talked about. My heart stopped.

The bell rang. When I jumped up, I bumped into the blabbermouth behind me. "Move!" I ran from the classroom.

The bathroom stall door slammed closed, and I plopped onto the seat. "Just because Momma's been acting crazy doesn't mean she's crazy. That's not what's wrong with her! She's not crazy. She's not crazy!" I rocked myself back and forth and buried my face in my hands. Finally, the banging in my chest, and the feeling like I was gonna puke, went away enough for me to leave.

I stalled as long as possible, hoping Miss Olivia would be done and gone from the locker next to mine. I yanked the science vocabulary test from my folder. The huge F stared back at me, like it was mocking me.

"Like I care." I wadded the paper and slammed it into the bottom of my locker to join the other bad grades and unfinished assignments.

"Kylie!"

Olivia! Ugh, where'd she come from?

"Gosh, Mr. Swan wasn't very happy with you when he passed back your test. What did you get?" She eyed the bottom of my locker.

"Mind your own business. Maybe it's because my mom's crazy," I said it half under my breath before I could stop it. I slammed my locker, hoping she didn't hear me—but knowing she did.

"That's not a nice thing to call your mom, Kylie!" Olivia said, with her voice not as screechy as usual.

She'd heard all right. I turned on her like a mad cat. "I didn't mean it! And you say it yourself about people!"

"I do not!"

"Yes, you do! I heard you talking about the lunch lady."

"I did not say that!" She marched away.

Well, that was nasty of me. Well, life's pretty nasty right now. What does she expect? I rubbed my aching temples. *But she doesn't know that.* "Olivia, I'm sorry," I hollered down the hall. I guess I should have been glad she had something else to find wrong with me besides losing the race last year.

You're getting pretty good at being a creep. I ducked into the bathroom again. *Like the other day, when you told Mom, "Just go lie down! I'll do it myself like I always do." Mom cries so often now, it almost annoys me. I hardly talk to Dad anymore. I don't want to be mad at him, but I am. The only times he's around is when she's doing well. Why can't he make Mom get better? Why can't he see it? I'm so tired of this; I just want things back like they were before.*

I stared at Joey on the bus ride home; I felt so zapped; it was an effort just to breathe. I wanted to smile at him and jab him with my pencil like usual, but I was just not up to it. I wanted to tell Joey about everything. I wanted to cry.

When Joey offered me his game player, I shook my head and looked away.

He watched me the rest of the way home; I could feel it. I made sure my eyes looked everywhere but into his, afraid I'd cry.

When I got off the bus at my lane, I heard the bus window screech down. I turned around, and Joey had his head stuck out.

"You sure you're okay, Kye?" he blurted out.

The last few kids on the bus gawked at me. I forced a smile to hide my embarrassment, and I shouted with as much sarcasm as I could find, "Now that I'm away from you I am!" I waved and turned to hurry up to the house.

Once inside, I slammed my backpack down on the table. I reached inside and pulled out the note from my English teacher. I opened and read. "Blah, blah, blah, we'd like to meet with you to discuss Kylie's lack of interest in her schoolwork this year." I ripped it up and reached for another paper. This one was the Math test with a big fat "F" on it.

Rip.

Next came a Science quiz with a "D-" and a note about the upcoming science fair project due in two weeks.

Rip. Rip.

I glanced at the mail that I'd also slammed on the table. The top letter was from the school principal. I ripped this one very small. Then, I buried all the shredded papers in the bottom of the trash. The red light on the answering machine blinked, so I pushed it to listen to the messages. It was the school office.

"Hello, we would like to meet with you at your convenience to discuss Kylie's schoolwork. Her grades have dropped drastically in most all of her classes, and her teachers are concerned. Please call me back to schedule a conference—"

"Ya, ya, ya. Like I have time to care about school anymore," I said as I pushed the delete button.

At the stairs, I listened for Mom. It was quiet upstairs, like always. So, I went up and sneaked past my parents' bedroom, then into the office.

Sitting at Dad's computer, I wrung my hands, while I stared at the blank screen. Do I really want to do this? I pressed my face hard into the palms of my hands. Finally, I shook myself out and sat up straight. "Okay. Here goes." I pulled up my favorite search engine and typed: "Symptoms moody, tired, sad, wired, shops, cleans." That ought to cover it.

I clicked on the first article, "Common Mental Health Diagnosis." The first chapter about depression sounded like Momma. The second chapter described bipolar disorder. My heart jerked when I recognized the symptoms. I quickly typed bipolar disorder into the search and scanned over as many articles about it as I could. They mostly all said the same thing.

"Bipolar Disorder, previously called Manic-Depressive Disease, is a mental illness that causes people to have severe high and low moods. People with this illness switch from feeling overly happy and joyful (or irritable) to feeling very sad.

"In between episodes of mood swings, a person may experience normal moods."

My palms felt sweaty. Sounds familiar. I took a slow, deep breath, trying to calm my racing heart, as I read on. The articles described the "manic" period.

"A person feels overly excited and confident, energetic and impulsive."

Like shopping all day, then baking brownies at 3AM?

"They can become irritable, angry and hostile and use bad judgment. Some patients even become psychotic, seeing and hearing things that aren't there."

Like thinking their kid's a thief. It was like my breath got caught in my lungs. I swallowed hard, 'cause I felt like my stomach was in my throat. Under the symptoms, I read:

"Uncontrollable crying, increased need for sleep, weight loss, not enjoying the same things they used to enjoy."

Like horses—like me?

I needed air. Mental disorder. Mental disorder. I squeezed my palms against my ears, trying to quiet the words in my head. When that didn't work, I clicked the X to clear the computer screen and ran off to the stable.

I went straight to Kiwi's stall, let myself in, and dropped into the pile of straw in the corner. A couple of stupid tears trickled down my cheeks. Kiwi turned toward me, flinching flies from her shoulders. I took a deep breath and wiped my tears away. *What's with all this crying crap? You big baby!* I wiped another tear and looked up to the cobwebbed rafters. My lips quivered. I gave in and cried. Kiwi moseyed over and nibbled on the brim of my cap, until it fell off my head.

I grabbed the horse blanket hanging on the wall above me and wiped it across my face. "What am I supposed to do now, huh, Kiwi?"

CHAPTER NINETEEN

I plopped on a bucket in Dad's shed.

"How about a 3/8 ratchet?" Dad asked.

"This one?" I handed the ratchet to him.

Dad clanked around under the truck awhile, then rolled out to look at me. "What are you doing sitting in here? Might be one of our last pretty fall days."

"Might be." I wobbled on my bucket. "Daddy, why don't we ever see Aunt Denise anymore?"

"I'm not real sure. I guess she and your mom just sort of grew apart. That happens sometimes."

I tried to find a way to word what I wanted to ask. "Well, is she like, okay?"

Dad looked at me funny. "Aunt Denise? I suppose she is. Something bugging you?"

"But, what if?"

He waited for me to finish.

"No. Nothing's bugging me."

"You sure? What if what?"

"I forgot what I was thinking. It must have been nothin'."

"Have you been feeling okay, kiddo?" Dad asked. "You're looking a little scrawny. You're not doing one of those weird cabbage and boiled egg diets, I hope."

"Gross, Dad. I'm fine."

"Why don't you get Joe and go out and get some air?"

Past the shed doors, the sun warmed the day. "Okay. See ya."

Joey never passed up a chance to go down by the lake, especially on his favorite trail. Noah Trail curved all through the woods, and then ended at the edge of the lake where you could fish from a picnic table. The trail kept going around the lake, looping in and out of the woods.

Joey and I bundled up for our walk. We knew the air would be crisp in the shade. We both loved walking through the crackling leaves and searching out fall colors. We sat in the sun by the lake to warm up and read our library books. Well, I pretended to read. Clouds, looking like cotton candy, cast shadows over the land of the Big Sky.

Dad was right. I did need to get outside. For a change, I put away the troubles I'd carried in my mind lately, and I tried to enjoy spending time with my friend.

"Why aren't you with O-liv-ee-AHHHHHHH?" I teased.

"I told you, I don't like Olivia!" Joey defended himself. "What do you care? I hear boys talking about you all the time. You know they like you."

"Yuck, Joey. They do not!"

Joey went back to his reading, but the pages in my book were just scattered words to me. Mom had seemed better the last few days, but what I'd read on the computer kept haunting me. Mental illness. Bipolar disorder. If that wasn't enough, I also kept wondering if the reason we never saw Aunt Denise was because she and Momma have the same problem. And if she's like that, too. Am I going to be that way when I'm older?

Lying in the sun next to Joey, I tried pretending to enjoy my book. The clouds gathered. As the sun lowered, my mood lowered. I had never felt as alone as I'd felt while keeping this secret. The secret about Momma. The secret about how day-by-day, she was turning into a stranger. I wished my heart was a rock— a rock wouldn't feel anything.

"Cool! Look at that!" said Joey.

The clouds had formed a giant crease across the sky. The sun sunk behind it, making the top clouds look a deep, dark gray. On each end of the crease, bright sunrays squeezed through and shone down on the land. The lake, centered between the rays, looked dark and lonely.

"Those are called crepuscular rays. We learned that in science." Joey squinted at the sunrays. "Doesn't that kinda remind you of God, the way those rays spread across the ground?"

I looked toward him, confused.

"Like the way God can keep an eye on one side of the world at the same time as He does on the other side."

I sighed. "You see that big dark spot on the lake, under those middle clouds?" I paused. "That's Momma. Right there, going crazy all alone. He's not watchin' over her."

Joey sat up, like when someone turns on the light in the morning. "What? What'd you say?"

I glared at him, my eyes full of tears and anger. I felt angry with myself for what again slipped out of my mouth. I felt angry with Mom for being crazy, or whatever she was. And I just now realized, I was struggling not to feel angry with God.

"Kye, what's wrong? What'd you mean?"

"Just never mind." I leapt up and ran.

Instead of backtracking to the trail, I kept going until I got to the lake's edge at the rocky side.

I can't believe that I said that to Joey. How the heck did that slip out? He can't keep a secret!

Parties, presents, passwords—forget it! Let alone this! Please, God, don't let everyone find out about Momma.

I sat on the rocks, stabbing a thin piece of driftwood into the ground. The ripples in the lake below overlapped each other; then they finally splattered over the rocks. I jammed the wood down into the dirt with such force that it snapped, then hurled it across the water. The stupid, hot tears began falling again. This time I gave in, and my shoulders shuddered with each sob until my head pounded. Leaves rustled near me, so I pulled my T-shirt collar up to wipe my eyes and nose.

"Hey," Joey greeted me.

I tried to steady my voice. "Hey."

Joey sat down next to me and began also digging in the dirt with a stick. For a long time, we didn't talk. We jumped when the gargled call of a Great Blue Heron broke the silence. The giant bird swooped low over the lake looking for fish, long legs trailing behind, gliding along with wings stretching wide. Like some prehistoric bird, it called again. We watched it swoop and scoop its head into the lake, then lift out a small wiggling fish in its beak.

"Cool."

"Yeah," I said, probably with no more enthusiasm than Joey.

Joey slowly scooted over, until we sat shoulder to shoulder. Quietly, we watched the sun set. Finally, Joey got up, offered me his hand and said, "Come on, Kye. Let's go home."

CHAPTER TWENTY

The phone rang and rang. On the tenth ring, the answering machine picked up the call. I listened to Joey's voice leaving the fourth message for me this weekend. I smashed the delete button and moped into the kitchen for a snack. I spotted Joey's school picture—with his one-eyed grin—hanging eye level on the refrigerator door.

I miss you, Joey. Sorry for not calling you back, and for ditching you on the bus and at school. But you'll make me talk. You'll keep bugging me about why I said, "She's going crazy." If you make me talk about it, I might cry again, and that does no good at all. Please don't hate me.

I yanked open the freezer door. The chilled air made me shiver. I wanted to crawl inside and ice my bad feelings until they were gone.

The summer flowers were drying, and leaves coated the ground in the woods. Specks of faded green peeked through the crisp brown grass in the yard. The scent of burning leaves drifted past, as Kiwi and I rounded the last barrel. "Yah! Yah! Yah!" We raced back to the finish line.

"Good girl, Kiwi. I think we were faster that time." Luckily, I had only missed a few weeks of training after my fall. Being back around Olivia at school made me all the more determined to work hard.

The stable doors banged open. I turned to see Mom wave on her way inside.

Well, God, she's up again. Please let her stay normal for a while. Kiwi and I rode on past the stable to check out where Dad burned leaves and tree trimmings.

"Hey, good morning." Dad tipped his hat. "How about you drag that hose over and dampen down this grass for me?"

"Sure." I tied Kiwi by the shed and returned to water the ground around the fire. How could I stay mad at my dad? Even though he was hardly ever around the house, all I had to do was come to the shed, or wherever he was, and he was still the same great dad he'd always been. Maybe it was best he stayed away from Mom since all they did lately was sneak away and argue when they were together.

"Got big plans for tomorrow? You know Mom's been feeling better. She really wants to go to the Fall Expo." Dad tossed some more branches onto the pile.

I jerked back when the wood popped a spark toward me.

"Why don't you call Joey to see if he wants to go along with you and Mom?" Dad grabbed the heavy end of a branch and crammed it farther into the flames. "I can't go. I promised Mr. Callaway I'd have his truck done, and I still have two in front of him to finish."

"I might be busy." I tucked my thumbs into my front pockets and looked down at the fire.

"Come on. It'd be good for you and Mom to spend some time together. Besides, you've worked so hard these past few months. Wouldn't it be nice to get away?"

"I don't know, Dad."

"You don't know what? You love the Expo."

I couldn't come up with an excuse fast enough. And he was right. It really would be good to do something fun. "All right, I'll call Joey later and see what he's doing tomorrow."

"Atta, girl." Dad hugged me then got back to his fire.

I sniffed my shoulder to see if the smoky smell on his jacket rubbed off onto me. "You're stinky!"

"Thanks. I love you, too."

After soaking the ground, I went inside to make the call. I stared at the phone, took a deep breath, and dialed. "Hey, Joe. I mean, Joey." I fidgeted with my earlobe. "My mom…um…my mom's…uh…she's better. I mean, she's doing really well…normal like." I looked at the ceiling. What am I saying? I paced the floor, while I stammered away. "Anyway, she wants to go to that big Fall Expo tomorrow. You probably don't want to go. You probably got plans already, but I thought if you wanted, to go, I mean, you could maybe go with us."

"The Expo! Are you serious?" Joey's voice rang in my ear. "I missed it last year. You bet I want to go. Let me ask my mom. Call you right back."

Before I could take a breath to answer, Joey hung up. I barely had hung up when he rang back, saying, "Cool! She said okay!"

We set a time to leave, and as soon as I hung up, I hoped it wasn't a mistake. I hated never knowing what the next day would be like with Momma.

I felt her warm hand on my shoulder. "What on earth are you doing all that pacing for? Something wrong?"

"Uh—no." I spun my thoughts for a believable answer to her question. "I guess I was just wondering what to wear to the Expo tomorrow. Joey's gonna come with us."

"Good! Did you just say you were worried about clothes? You sure you're feeling okay?" She lifted my curls away from my face and felt my forehead. Our eyes met, and she winked at me.

The question is: are you going to feel okay tomorrow? I searched Mom's eyes.

The next morning, our truck rocked up Joey's lane. From the porch, I could see Joey's dad eyeing the horse trailer that Mom had insisted on towing. "Well, looks like you're planning on buying 'em out," he hollered to Momma.

Joey charged out of the house.

"Hey, bud. Come here." Joey's dad teased him by grabbing him in a wrestling hold around the neck. "You leave some of the food at the concessions for the others. Will ya?" Then he rubbed his knuckles on Joey's head, leaving his hair looking like a bird's nest.

"Cut it out!" Joey pulled away to climb into the back seat. He looked at the huge trailer behind us, then he looked at me with questions in his eyes.

I shrugged my shoulders and shook my head.

Joey leaned forward to greet Mom. "Morning, Mrs. Hannigan!"

"Hi, pal. Get you up early enough?"

"That's okay. I'm all psyched that I get to go this year. We gonna watch the rodeo?"

"You two can."

My shoulders relaxed, seeing Joey's ease with Mom. Especially after what I had said about her at the lake.

I distracted myself by thinking about the rodeo. Joey loved calf roping. But I hated to watch when a little calf staggered out of the chute looking bewildered at the crowd. Then, hearing pounding hooves, the scared baby saw the roper coming out of a cloud of dust with a lasso flying towards his neck. I could almost hear him moo, "Oh crap!" before he made a run for it.

On the way to the Expo, the sun broke through the dawn and shimmered on the few leftover leaves, showing off their colors. At least God gave us a beautiful day for a long drive.

I entered the Expo gates with Mom and Joey. The familiar commotion of the visitors and vendors gave me a rush of good feelings. "Thank you, God," I murmured.

We walked for over an hour. We checked out the exhibits, picked through tables of tack, and admired show saddles and other horse stuff. Joey picked up brochures from the cattle breeder's tent, and I tried on cowboy hats from an unbelievable selection of styles. Mostly, we watched Joey eat everything in sight.

"Where are you putting all that?" I asked.

"All wha'?" Joey asked with half a corndog crammed in his mouth.

Mom and I laughed. We passed a live band and could feel the music's vibrations. Mom grabbed Joey's hand and pulled him over for a quick spin to a classic country song. His cheeks turned pink, but he danced along and even dipped her at the end of the song.

Several area ranchers recognized Mom on the way to the livestock show.

"You taking those two young'uns to the auction to see what they'll go for?" teased one man.

"Nope. These two are keepers!" Mom said.

We passed Mr. Riley. "How's that concussion, Kylie?"

"Much better, thank you."

"You finding enough to eat, Joey?" he asked, then winked at me.

"Yes, sir. They made me take a break, though."

We reached the booth selling rodeo tickets.

"Okay, you two. Here are your rodeo tickets. You remember where the cowboy hats were?" Mom asked.

We nodded.

"Meet me there at 6:30. Gosh, you need a week to see all this! 6:30, okay? Cowboy hats. Don't forget! Enjoy the rodeo."

"Okay, Mom, thanks." I felt a pang of worry, remembering this morning when Dad warned Mom to watch her spending.

"And Kye, no rooting for the calf." Mom joked, as she disappeared into the crowd.

Joey looked at me. "The calf? What's wrong with you?" He reached over and pulled my hat down over my eyes.

Throughout the horse show, I "oohed and aahed" along with the crowd. I longed to take each horse home with me. I sat on my hands during the calf roping event and hid my flinches every time a calf was slammed to the ground and hogtied. But I secretly cheered when a calf escaped the roper. We cheered and screamed for the barrel racers. And we jumped out of our seats when any cowboy got bucked off his bronco.

After the rodeo, we made our way down the stairs of the grandstand.

"I'm glad you invited me today, Kye. I've kind of been missing you."

I leaned over and bumped shoulders with him. "Yeah, me too."

It was 6:20 when we found the vendor with the cowboy hats and an empty seat on a bench, where we could people watch while we waited for Mom.

"Look, there you are," I said, motioning to a man carrying cotton candy in one hand and cradling fries and hotdogs in the other.

"Thanks a lot."

The crowd moved toward the gate. Some people were lugging hats, bridles, saddle blankets, and branding irons. Others lined up at the claim tent to pick up their bigger stuff.

"Where do you think my mom's at?"

"What time is it?" Joey asked.

"6:55, she's not usually this late."

"Hey, here comes Mr. Hanley."

"Mr. Hanley, have you seen my mom?" I asked a rancher Mom had worked for last summer.

"Well, I saw her about thirty minutes ago at the auction. She was bidding pretty heavy on the horses," he answered.

"Thanks, thanks a lot." I stared at the ground a minute. The worry from earlier flew back. So I jumped up. "I gotta go find her, Joey."

"Hey, wait. I'm coming with you."

We wove through the crowd, looking for the auction arena. When we found it, there were hundreds of people crammed inside.

"Come on, Kylie, we'll never find her. Let's go back and wait."

"No, you don't get it. I have to find her!" I shoved past Joey, searching up and down the rows of people. Finally, over on the other side of the arena and close to the front, I spotted Mom.

People stood shoulder to shoulder. I squeezed through, ducked under, whatever it took to get to Mom fast. "Here you are. We've been waiting. Mom, it's 7:15!"

"Shh!" She waved me away, looking around me to the auctioneer.

"6:30, remember? We were worried."

Joey caught up and found a spot close by.

"Kylie, hush! I can't hear the bids."

"Im'a bid seven four. Seven four. Seven thousand four hundred dollars to the man in the red vest. Wud'bout seven five? Seven five? Seven thousand five hundred dollars? D'I hear seven thousand five?" the auctioneer chanted.

Mom raised her bidding paddle.

"Seven thousand five to the lady in the front. Im'a bid seven thousand five hundred. D' I hear seven thousand six hundred? Seven six? D'I hear seven six? Im'a bid seven five. D'I hear seven six?"

I searched around, praying for another bidder. The rapid firing of the auctioneer's chant sung in the background. I leaned close to Mom and lowered my voice, so Joey couldn't hear. "Momma, what are you doing?"

"I'm trying to buy that beauty up there if you'll sit quiet and stay out of my way."

"But, Momma, you promised Daddy. I heard you."

"Seven thousand six hundred! Im'a bid seven thousand six hundred to the man in the red vest. D'I hear seven thousand seven hundred?" the auctioneer picked up his chants a notch.

"Momma! That's almost eight thousand dollars for a horse. We've never spent that on a horse! Come on, I want to go home." I grabbed her arm as I got up and turned to leave, but she yanked away and raised her paddle again.

"Seven thousand seven hundred dollars to the lady. Im'a bid seven seven, lucky sevens. D'I hear seven thousand eight hundred dollars? Seven eight? Seven eight? D'I hear seven thousand eight hundred dollars?"

I looked for the man in the red vest. *Please God, let him bid again. Please, God!* I found him in the middle section a few rows behind us. *Bid again, mister. Come on, mister, bid again.* My head rang from the speed of the auctioneer's voice. I remembered Dad this morning telling Mom, "Promise me, you'll only pick up a little tack that we need. I can't start getting into our savings to pay off any more of your shopping debts."

Finally, the man slowly raised his paddle, and I could breathe again.

"Momma, come on, let him have her. You've got plenty of horses. Please, Momma, Daddy's gonna be so mad. Please!"

"I'm gonna be the one so mad if you don't get away from me and mind your business!"

Even with the noise of the crowd, people heard her and turned to stare. "But, Mom—"

"But nothing, young lady. Who do you think you are coming up here telling me how I can spend my money, and in front of all these people? What's gotten into you, Kylie? You're lucky there are all these people around because if we were alone I'd—"

"Going twice. SOLD to the man in the red vest!" The hammer fell. "Swift Whiskey Filly, sold for seven thousand eight hundred dollars!"

The look in Mom's eyes turned me cold.

"Look what you've done! There were more than ten people bidding on that horse. It finally got down to just me and that man. I would have had her if you hadn't come along distracting me." She shoved past me and headed for the door.

I just stood there, frozen from Mom's icy words. Joey walked to me from his spot at the end of the aisle, where he had heard the whole mess, took my arm, and led me after Mom. We walked to the truck without speaking.

After we got into the truck, Mom got in and slammed the door, squealed the tires, and came to a screeching halt at the claim tent. I saw the handful of claim tickets she held and felt my chest tighten again. Everything got thrown into the trailer, and I wondered how much she had spent. Again, the door slammed, and we flew through the parking lot.

"Careful, Momma, there are people walking."

She ignored me. When we got on the hard road she accelerated, the trailer wove behind us.

"Whoa," Joey mumbled from the back seat.

"Momma, please slow down. Remember you're pulling a trailer." I kept my voice low.

"Quiet, Kylie. You're already in enough trouble. What's wrong with you anyway? You used to like to go fast," Mom said, lips pursed, face flushed.

"Not while pulling a horse trailer on a curvy road!"

I looked back apologetically at Joey.

He smiled a little and shrugged his shoulders.

I tightened my seatbelt and tried to sit still, so as not to irritate her any further.

Mom flew around semi trucks in no passing zones and honked at cars in her way. She whipped around a car so fast that we went over the shoulder of the road.

"Geez." Joey turned to watch out the back window.

I heard horns blast.

Mom jerked the wheel to get the truck and trailer back on the road, but then we flew over into the other lane of traffic, facing a Peterbilt head on.

Joey and I screamed. "Momma, look out!" I covered my face.

Bwaawwww! The deep sounding horn blared, as the semi-truck missed us by only inches.

"Slow down! You are scaring me and Joey. I'm sorry,-I'm sorry for whatever I did, but please slow down! Momma, please," I begged.

"Oh, Shut up! I could've had that horse. One more bid, and I would've had her. Don't you see? If you hadn't distracted me. It's your fault, Kylie. It's all your fault!" Mom shouted, then looked confused.

"I'm sorry, Momma. I didn't mean to, really. Just slow down a little, just a little. People are honking. Someone's going to call the police."

"The police?" Mom glanced down at the speedometer and eased her foot from the gas. I saw her look in the rearview mirror, so I turned and saw Joey all wide-eyed. Mom sat up straight, gripped the wheel tight, and thank God, she slowed down. She turned at the next intersection and pulled over at the first gas station.

We waited without a word. Mom took shaky, deep breaths, staring straight ahead. Her hands clung tight on the steering wheel.

"I just need to get out for a minute. You two go on in, if you want, and get yourselves a soda." Her voice cracked, and she trembled as she slowly got out of the car.

Joey and I watched her walk past the station to a clearing and beyond.

"What's she gonna do?" Joey asked.

"I have no idea."

"Kylie, what's your dad gonna say about this?"

"Nothing. He says nothing. They used to fight about the way she's been acting. But now he just hides in the shop all the time."

Joey waited for me to go on.

"Joey, I shouldn't have said that about her the other day. You know, about her being crazy. Olivia and her friend were talking about the lunch lady acting crazy. And, what they said about the way she was, well, she sounded just like…my mom. At least the way she's been lately."

I climbed into the back seat with Joey. "I went home and searched up her symptoms to try and prove Momma's not crazy. I read about this thing called bipolar disorder. It said people with it switch between feeling really great to feeling really low. I don't know if that's what's wrong with her or not. I just want her back the way she used to be. I've been trying to figure out a way to help her. You gotta promise, Joey. Promise you won't tell anyone!"

"I promise. I swear I won't tell anyone. But you gotta talk to your dad, Kylie. You gotta tell him about today. She coulda killed us! Not on purpose, I mean. You know what I mean. You gotta tell him; maybe he'll know how to help her."

"Do you think he knows what's wrong with her? Does he think she's crazy, too, and that's why he spends all his time outside in the shed?" I asked.

"I don't know. At least now I get it. I mean, why you don't talk to anyone at school. Why you look like you never sleep. Dang, Kye."

"First she's good. Then she's bad again; then she sleeps all the time. Then she's all wacky like today. But I can't tell anyone. I can't have anyone bad-mouth Momma like those kids did the lunch lady!" I rubbed my face. "Remember that camp we went to? Remember the basketball player that gave that big talk and all? He said that God knows we can't handle things on our own, so he sends us a team. That team, they work together to figure things out. Remember?"

"Yeah, I remember."

"I don't have a team, Joey. It's just me. And I don't know what to do." I looked out the window, my eyes full of tears. "He said God is the team captain. Where was God today? Huh, Joey?"

Joey stared out his window. "Maybe, Kye, maybe He was pulling our truck back on the road, outta the way of that semi."

"Maybe."

"Maybe He was trying to convince you to ask me and your dad to join your team."

"Yeah, maybe."

"And if you want, my mom and dad, too. Only if you want." Joey reached over and took my hand. "Don't cry. It's gonna be okay."

"I'm not crying. Well, maybe, just a little." I leaned over and wiped my nose on the sleeve of my first team member and best, best friend.

CHAPTER TWENTY-ONE

I stayed in the back seat with Joey on the long drive home from the Expo. Mom didn't try to start a conversation. She just drove. Drove really nice and slowly. After dropping Joey off at his house, she turned and asked me, "You want to come up here, Sunshine?"

"Nah, we'll be home here quick. I'm okay."

When we pulled up to the house, the headlights shone on Dad sitting in the rocker on the porch. He had a pile of papers on his lap and a mad look on his face. *Uh oh, must have found some more credit card bills. Look out, Mom.* The old porch creaked when Dad greeted us on the steps. I heard a stereo chorus of cicadas from trees all around the house. Rheee-urr-rheee-urr-rheee.

"We need to talk," Dad spoke to me—not Mom.

I looked down to the pile of papers he held and saw it—my report card.

"We're tired. Whatever it is can wait." Mom patted him on the shoulder and tried to pass.

"No, this is not going to wait."

"I'm going to bed. I can't concentrate on anything right now."

"Me too, Dad. I'm pooped."

Dad's face hardened. "Sit! Both of you."

We crept over to the swing and sat as ordered.

"This is Kylie's report card." He waved the top paper at us. "It was hand delivered by Principal Collins today. Seems they've been trying to get a hold of us to discuss Kylie's behavior and her schoolwork. They've sent home notes, left phone messages, even mailed letters."

I twisted my hair around my finger and looked at the ground. I could feel Dad's eyes on me, like the sun caught in a magnifying glass.

"Kylie, is there some problem with our answering machine?"

"Uh…no, sir. Not that I know of."

"Do you think the mail carrier forgot to deliver those letters? Seems I remember you've been bringing up the mail."

"I guess, not likely," I mumbled.

Dad shoved the papers under my nose. "These are Fs, Kylie, every one of them! Your teachers told Mr. Collins that you haven't turned any papers in until the past few weeks. And even those showed little effort."

"I—," I started to talk but Mom interrupted.

"Leave her alone! We've had an awful day. Can't you tell? I can't think about this right now. I need to go to bed!"

"Just go to bed, Momma. Like always!" I exploded. "And don't bother telling him about why our day was awful. Don't tell him about all the things you bought today after you promised not to. And don't tell him how you almost KILLED me and Joey!"

I turned to Dad. "Ask her about the semi! Look in the trailer, Dad. And maybe if you'd spend some time up at the house instead of hiding in your shop all the time, maybe you'd see why I haven't been doing my homework!"

"Stop it!" Mom begged with tears in her eyes.

I slammed my hands down on the swing, then I jumped up and ran into the house. I heard Mom following me up the stairs, but I ran to my room and threw myself on the bed and buried my face in the pillow. I lay there expecting to hear Mom's voice; instead, I only heard my parents' bedroom door click closed. I felt like I'd been ripped in half and thrown in the dirt.

Footsteps thumped slowly up the old stairs, and they paused at my doorway. "Can I come in?" Dad asked. When I didn't answer, he came over and sat on the edge of the bed. "What happened, Kye? Talk to me."

I turned away from Dad and talked to the wall. "Today started really good. We were having fun. But

137

then I found her at the horse auction. Daddy, you won't believe how high she was bidding on this horse. When I said something about you getting mad, she exploded! She yelled at me in front of Joey and everyone. Then she drove like some, well, she drove so fast I thought she was gonna kill us! Really! Dad, she about slammed us into a semi! Ask Joey."

I finally faced Dad. My tears soaked my face, my nose dripped, and my voice cracked, but I kept going until I got it all out. "Daddy, something's really wrong with her, and you know it!"

He looked away from me.

"I'm just a kid, but even I know that people don't sleep for weeks. And they don't ignore their family and their horses and their house. I tried to help. Even I couldn't stand the mess. She was so sad; I thought it would help if she didn't have to look at all the work.

"Then Momma was okay for a while. But all of a sudden, she never slept. She was cleaning like crazy. You remember? And cooking—it's not normal to cook everything in the kitchen for one meal. And what about the makeup? You had to notice that! She probably spent more on makeup than she spends on groceries."

Dad took a deep breath. He leaned over his knees, face in his hands.

"Do you even know how lonely I've been? Momma's been either sleeping, working, or shopping. I miss her so bad. I miss Momma, the old Momma.

And I miss you! When you did act like you cared, you'd argue with her. I felt like that was my fault. Then you just hid in the shop with your head under a hood, leaving me alone to figure out what was wrong with her."

I wiped my nose on my shirt. "I've been so mad. Mad at both of you for not being here for me anymore."

Dad handed me his hanky.

I hiccupped a sob. "I would just get used to her being awake, and she'd start sleeping again all the time. Daddy, the reason I didn't do my homework at first, was because someone had to do the chores. Someone had to do the laundry. Someone had to cook. Did you think Mom was cooking supper all that time?" I sat up and turned to look at him. "I'm used to doing my chores and all, but I'm not used to being Momma. I've been training that foal, too. And trying to work barrels with Kiwi. And don't forget Dragonfly. She should have had him trained months ago. Who do you think talked Mr. Jinks into giving us more time with him? Wasn't Momma!"

"Kylie, I thou—"

"I don't have any time for figuring math or reading history. I don't care anymore! When I try to think about schoolwork, all I do is think about Momma and wonder how long she's gonna act this way." I paused, then I finally looked at him. "I tried to talk to you."

"You haven't said anything about school."

"Not about school, about Mom!"

Dad scooped me up and held me tight. "I'm sorry, Kylie. You're right. I was afraid something was wrong with Mom. I couldn't get her to go to the doctor. When I tried to talk to her about it, we'd only fight. I grew up listening to my parents fight all the time, and I didn't want that for you. I figured I was more of a problem than she was, so I stayed away and made excuses for her when I could. I wanted to help her, Kye. But I just didn't know how. So, I hid in the shop and buried myself in my work, so I didn't have time to worry about it."

I got up and dug in the bottom of a drawer and handed him the copies I'd made from the website about bipolar disorder. "Do you think this is what's wrong with her? If it is, doctors can help her."

"Bipolar disorder...manic depressive...mental disorder," Dad read.

We stopped when we heard sobbing. It was Momma, leaning against my doorframe with her hands covering her face. "I'm sorry. I'm so sorry."

CHAPTER TWENTY-TWO

Thank God, it was a cool morning. I could sit with my head down, and my hood pulled over my face, so that no one on the bus would try to talk to me. My eyes teared up when I thought about how Momma cried last night, as she told Daddy what happened. She had looked at me and said, "When I looked over and saw the look on your face, and the fear in Joey's eyes in the mirror, it scared me so bad. I don't know what's wrong with me. I need to go see Doc."

The school bus groaned to a halt at Joey's lane. He boarded and moved my backpack to sit down next to me. Joey leaned close to my ear and asked, "So, what happened?"

I pulled off my hood since I could barely hear him over the noise from the bus. Mom had wanted Dad to call Joey's parents last night to explain and to make sure he was okay. But I wasn't sure what he had told them. "What do you mean?"

"Last night! Your dad called really late and talked to my dad forever. Our names kept coming up. But he was talking too low. Did you tell him?"

"Did I ever." I looked away, then looked back at him. "Mom heard. She heard it all. We didn't know she was there."

"What're ya gonna do?"

"You get your report card?" I asked.

"Yeah. Come on; don't change the subject."

"The principal brought mine to my dad yesterday." I grabbed the top of the seat in front of me and dropped my head. "I got all Fs."

"Fs'! In everything?"

"Shhh. Everything. Even P.E."

"P.E!" Joey tried to whisper. "How the heck do you flunk P.E.?"

"I seriously didn't know that was possible either. Dad called the principal last night, too. He told Dad he would set up a meeting with the social worker for after school today. Funny, Mom's the one with the problem, but I gotta talk to the social worker." I fumbled with the strap of my backpack. "We go see Doc Jordan on Thursday. Mom realized something was wrong when she about splattered us into that semi truck. She even asked Dad to call the doc."

"Good; that's good."

"Were you scared?" I asked.

"When?"

"Come on. When we thought we were gonna become roadkill?"

"Oh, nah. Yeah, a little." Joey's cheeks turned pink, and he turned to the window.

"A little? You were crappin'. I know you."

"What about you?" Joey asked.

"Are you kidding? I could see that guy's eyes. We were so close. I could see his dang eyes! I thought we were dead! No kidding. I bet that guy had to pull over and clean himself up!"

Our eyes met, and Joey snorted out a laugh. I joined in, and we laughed so hard the bus driver looked in the mirror to check on the commotion. When we saw him looking, we tried to be quiet, but that just made us laugh harder. I don't know what I would do without Joey. Laughing with him pushed out some of the bad feelings I'd been filled with and finally let back in a little bit of happy.

God, I am so ready for this day to be over with.

Finally, the bell rang, and the hallways buzzed with kids rushing to their lockers to unload and load up again for the night.

On his way to the bus, Joey walked me to the library, where I was to wait for my parents. "Good luck."

"Thanks." I peeked into the empty room, then watched him walk away.

My footsteps echoed down the aisles of the deserted library, as I made my way to the back of the room. Waiting at a table, I tried to work on a math paper. I worked the same problem five times and got a different answer every time. The same thought kept interrupting my concentration—*I bet it'll just be Daddy. Momma's not going to show up. Or worse, what will she be like if she does?* I slammed my pencil on the table, then laid my head on my folded arms.

"Hey, Sunshine," whispered Mom.

It was all I could do not to jump up and run to her and Dad.

"Are you ready?" Dad checked his watch. "You know the way, so we'll follow you."

I looked down at my trembling hands. "Am I going to get in trouble?"

Dad crouched down and looked me in the eyes. "No way, kiddo. You had plenty of reason to not do well in school and try to hide it. But we've got some fixing to do." He looked up at Mom. "All of us together. So, come on. How about we go find Mrs. Welling and get this part over?"

While we waited outside the office, I wondered how much Principal Collins had told Mrs. Welling of the late-night phone call from Dad yesterday. I had laid awake all night, wishing I hadn't told Dad everything, wishing I hadn't shown him the information about bipolar. Did he tell Principal Collins about that also? A new fear crept over me. Fear that my classmates would find out about my mom being mentally ill—if that's what she was. They might learn I had to go see the social worker. I imagined kids circling around me, teasing, "I heard your mom's crazy! Are you crazy, too?"

Why didn't I just act like nothing happened, like I've been doing? I should have told Momma not to worry about almost killing us. I should have said that I hated school this year, so I didn't care that I was flunking, even P.E. Then, just took my punishment. That's what I should have done.

Dad laid his hand on my shoulder, and I tried to calm my jittering knees. I imagined the woman behind the door as a tall, husky woman with a gruff voice. She was gonna glare down at me to make sure I knew how bad I messed up. I wondered how Mom could sit there so calmly, staring at the floor. Will the social worker ask her questions? Is Momma going to be in trouble? Dad said I wouldn't get in trouble, but what if he's wrong? What if I get kicked out of school and can never come back?

Finally, the door opened, and Mrs. Welling introduced herself.

I had passed her office before, but this was the first time I'd really seen her. She was just the opposite of what I had imagined all day. Mrs. Welling had kindness in her face. She was only a little taller than me. If this were a normal day, something about her would have set me at ease. But, right now, not knowing what to expect, I was miles away from at ease. We took seats inside the small office.

"Mr. Collins filled me in on what has been going on, Kylie."

My heart sprung into quadruple speed. I snuck a quick look at Mom, wondering if she was mad at me for telling, mad at me that now everyone knew. What would I do if this woman began saying I had a horrible mom?

"We're going to help you get caught up on your schoolwork. We'll work with your teachers and ask them to let you start making up assignments and re-taking tests."

Mom took my hand and squeezed it. I waited for the bad part of this meeting to happen.

"Kylie, you and your parents have taken the first step. I know this wasn't easy. You should be very proud of yourselves. I understand your mom hasn't met with her doctor yet, so you must be feeling very confused. Maybe nervous?"

I nodded. *Petrified,* I thought to myself.

"The reason you are meeting with me already, Kylie, is so you'll know that I am here for you. You have been through a lot, and sometimes, it's good just to have someone to talk with. I'm going to schedule times for you to come here during the lunch break. But please, come see me anytime."

I stared at my lap and picked at the dry cuticles around my fingernails. "You mean, I'm not in trouble?"

Mrs. Welling looked at me and then at my parents. "No, Kylie. You are not in one bit of trouble. I'm here to, hopefully, help things get better for you—not worse."

"But, how will I ever get all caught up and do the new work, too?"

"It's still early in the year. You're smart, Kylie. Mr. Collins told me that normally you are a very good student. I'm sure you can do it. If by the end of the year, you're still having trouble? Don't worry. There is always summer school," said Mrs. Welling.

I wanted to look at Mom and Dad to see their reaction to what she said. But I was afraid I might sob in relief, so I kept working on my fingers.

As we left Mrs. Welling's office, I watched the ground and bit the inside of my cheek, the way I'd done since I was little when I was upset. Dad held the outside door for us, but when I passed, he took my arm and pulled me close.

"I know that you did a good job of hiding what was going on at school from us. But I should have seen it. I should have known what you were going through, both of you, and stepped in sooner. I don't know if it would have done any good or not. But I'm really sorry," Dad said.

"I know, Dad. I'm sorry, too, for hiding my work and all the notes, and for deleting the phone messages from school." I leaned my head into Dad's chest, and I looked at Mom. She stood next to us with her shoulders drooped, like she had already lost the fight. "I love you, Momma." I turned and wrapped my arms around her for a long hug while my tears soaked her blouse.

CHAPTER TWENTY-THREE

Little things got better every day after the Expo. Mom's illness and all my cover-up were finally out in the open. I prayed that I would get my normal mom back, though it couldn't be fast enough for me.

I sat cross-legged on the living room floor with homework spread over the coffee table and beside me on the carpet.

Dad looked up from reading the newspaper in the recliner. "Switch to the news. Will ya? You've got the TV remote buried somewhere in that mess."

"Dad! You keep bugging me, and I'm shipping you back to the shop," I teased.

Mom came from the kitchen and plopped next to Dad. The smell of bleach lingered after her. "I'm finished in there. I want to go lie down so bad. I'll try hard to stay up a while longer with you two though."

I couldn't keep from smiling. *Wow, God, all three of us in the same room in the evening. Amazing!*

Saturday morning, I rode Kiwi over to Joey's house. His mom nearly knocked me over at the doorway, hugging me so tight.

"Get in here, Punkin. Joey's finishing his breakfast. You pull up a chair, and I'll get you a plate. Don't you even think about saying no! You look like you're gonna blow away. I'll make you three—three big, chocolate chip pancakes."

At the table, I pushed Joey's hair down so both eyes were covered instead of just the one. When I sat down, Mrs. McLagan pulled a chair over close to me.

"Now, honey, I want you to know that Joey's dad and I have been talking to your mom and dad this week. We've been praying our hearts out for all of ya. Anytime, I mean anytime, you want someone to talk to, please, please, call us. Anytime, you hear me! You know how much I love your mom, and I love you like you're my own. It's gonna be okay. There may be bumps along the way, but God's gonna get you through this."

I leaned my head on Joey's mom's plump shoulder and swiped away the tear that snuck from my eye. "Thanks. I love you, too."

The smell of burnt batter filled the room. "Oh, now I went and burned your pancakes!"

Joey saddled Butch in the stable after breakfast. "Dad wants me to ride down to the bottom land and move the herd over to the pasture along the river. You coming?"

"Sure, I'll get Kiwi." I stepped outside as the breeze shifted. The strong odor of cow manure hit me in the face. "Uck. I'm so glad that we have horses."

"What?" Joey hollered as he led Butch from the stable.

"Nothing. Just talking to Kiwi." I looked at Kiwi. "Shhh."

We rode side by side across the golden pasture, slowly dipping down to the bottom acreage, where one of many herds of Joey's red- and white-faced Hereford cattle grazed.

"Did it go all right with Doc Jordan?" Joey asked hesitantly.

"I guess so. He said the hardest part was realizing we needed help." I pulled my curls up and through the hole in the back of my cap. "He's sweet, ol' Doc is. He hugged Mom, told her he was proud of her coming to see him."

"Yeah, he's cool."

"After we all talked, Dad and I went out, so he could talk to just Mom. When we came back, he said he thinks that Mom has bipolar disorder, going by what we all told him. He ran some tests to rule out other things." I looked at Joey and shook my head. "For once, I didn't want to be right."

"Yeah, really," Joey agreed.

"He made an appointment with some special doctor in Billings. They went yesterday. I couldn't miss school."

"What'd that guy say?" Joey nudged Butch to catch up with me.

Butch snorted and shook his bridle.

"Mom said, he asked her a million questions, looked at all her test results, and then agreed with Doc Jordan. He gave her some medicine and a bunch of stuff to read. She'll have more appointments with him." We rode a while longer. "Do you think I'll get it, Joey? I read it can be hereditary. I don't want to get it."

"You're not going to get it."

"Whoa." I stopped Kiwi. "What am I gonna do, Joey? Hi, I'm Kylie Hannigan, and I might just go crazy someday. Nice to meet ya."

"Well, you say that, and they'll figure you're already there," Joey kidded me.

Leaves blew across the trail. A rabbit zigzagged through the tall dry grass, not knowing whether to race in front of the horses or behind.

"Doc wants me to meet with Mrs. Welling once a week or so at school. That's just what I need. Someone will see me going in there. I just know it."

"So? It's nobody's business."

"Yeah, so, they'll make it their business. And if they can't find out why I'm talking to her, they'll make something up."

"Sounds to me like your mom's just sick, and you need someone to talk to while she gets better."

We reached the bottom ground and separated to start rounding up the cattle. Kiwi instinctively circled the herd, cutting around the stragglers. We worked well together. Soon, we had all the cattle grouped to begin moving them over to the next pasture of clover for late season grazing.

Leaving the moaning cattle behind us, we started back to Joey's house.

"What a shame you have so many chores waiting for you," I smirked. "Dad gave me the day off, except for homework."

"Good, you can help me then."

"Forget it."

"Hey, you're the one who showed up at chore time. Come on."

"All right, but only if you'll help me with my homework."

"Deal."

We rode the long way back, slow and easy. I felt sort of limp, like maybe it was okay now to let a little happy slide back in again.

CHAPTER TWENTY-FOUR

I looked from my window. The sun warmed the glass. Last night, the weatherman said it would be sunny but a little chilly today. Perfect riding day. I watched Mom walk past and wanted to ask her to join me for a ride, but something held me back. Mom's mood seemed to be leveling out. But what if—oh, just stop! "Momma, you feel up to a ride today?"

Mom agreed on a ride down Noah Trail. It felt so good to get out of the stuffy house.

I placed the rolled-up comforter in the front of my saddle to use at the lake. It should be comfortable sitting by the water, even with the slight breeze.

As Kiwi followed Mom and Josie, I listened for scurrying animals. It was a different trail when the leaves had fallen, and you could see through the trees. Deer blended into their surroundings making it hard to spot them. Squirrels were busy gathering food for the winter. Aside from the horses snorting, and the

155

sound of crunching leaves under their hooves, I heard peaceful silence.

When we reached the lake, we tied the horses to a tree. Mom took a seat next to me at the picnic table and wrapped the comforter over our shoulders. She poured cups of steamy apple cider from a thermos, and then pulled a bag of raisin-oatmeal cookies from her coat pocket. "This is nice." Mom took a sip of cider and leaned her head toward me until our curls met.

"Momma, can I ask you something?"

She searched my eyes. "Anything."

"When I used to hear you crying at night, I always wondered what made you so sad. I mean, I know you were sick. But...did something start it, the sadness?"

Mom thought for a moment. "I don't know." She stared at the water and chewed a bite of her cookie, then swallowed. "I mean, it's hard to explain. Just being made me sad. At first, I just got so tired. I would start out to work with the horses. But by the time I got on my boots and got half across the yard, my legs felt so heavy that I thought I wouldn't make it to the barn. Some days, I'd make myself go—get little things done; other days, I'd just turn around, go inside, and take a nap."

She swirled the cider in her cup. "I remember standing at the sink, looking at the dirty dishes. I'd think, I can't do it. I am never going to get them done. We have a dishwasher for crying out loud! It wasn't like I'd be standing at the sink with my hands in hot water for an hour washing dishes. But still, the thought of doing those dishes was so overwhelming." Mom shook her head. "That sounds silly. Huh?"

I shrugged my shoulders.

Mom tucked the blanket over me again and went on. "When you and Dad were out, and the house got quiet, this feeling, this sadness, would overcome me. I didn't know why, and that made it worse. I'd talk to myself—you have such a blessed life; what is there to be sad about? I'd get all teary again. I wanted so bad to be happy. Everyday felt like a black hole that kept getting bigger, sucking me in. I'd lie in bed not wanting to get up because I'd have to face the feelings I was having. Sleeping was the only way to get relief."

I decided to keep my thoughts to myself. I sniffed the spicy cider from the warm cup in my hands, thinking: *Why didn't you just tell me? Why'd you shut me out? Why'd you make me feel like it was me making you cry?*

Mom peeled back the splintering wood on the picnic table and stacked the tiny pieces in a pile. "Then, the fog would lift for a while. I'd start thinking clearly, and I could face the days again.

"But, after a while, just feeling good wasn't enough. I wanted to feel great, look great, be great. I wasn't happy with having a clean house. The house had to be immaculate. The more I was able to accomplish in one day, the more powerful I felt. I was so full of these perfect ideas, and I was so frustrated there weren't enough hours in the day to pursue them. I could feel again." Mom reached for the curl that had fallen into my face and smoothed it into the other curls.

"I got more and more frustrated, and the ideas would race through my brain getting scrambled. I couldn't sleep. I couldn't turn off my head." Mom stopped and looked at me. "Oh well, that's enough of that."

"Your medicine is working now. Right?" I asked.

Mom rubbed my back and said, "It's working. Thank God. And riding and just being around the horses help calm me now. I'm getting cold. How about you? Ready to head back?"

While we rode home, I processed everything Mom had said, and a tear trickled down my cheek. *It wasn't me, God. She couldn't help it; she tried to be happy.* I breathed in deeply and let myself exhale my anger about Momma.

CHAPTER TWENTY-FIVE

I was finally feeling comfortable talking with the social worker at our lunchtime meetings.

"But, Mrs. Welling, what if the kids find out? What if they find out I have to talk to you because my mom went mental? I've heard the way they talk about people."

"Why do you think the kids talk about people with illnesses?" Mrs. Welling asked.

"Because they're stupid! And mean." I looked at the clock, then listened for kids outside the door.

"We'll talk more about this next week, Kylie."

The school bell rang.

I left Mrs. Welling's office and headed for my locker.

"Ky-leeee!"

My breath caught in my chest, but I kept walking. After many times meeting at our locker, and her not talking to me, she must have forgiven me now.

"Hey, Ky-leeee!" Olivia strutted up to me. "Did you just come out of Mrs. Welling's office?"

"Um, yeah."

"I thought so. I..."

"Yeah," I interrupted. "Uh...I found out she's good friends with . . . my aunt's . . . neighbor. And, I needed to talk to her to see if she knew my aunt fell—and if she had heard how she was doing."

Olivia looked disappointed. "Oh."

She paused. Almost like she wanted to tell me something. After a super awkward minute, she held up her lunch sack. "Well, I gotta get back to the cafeteria. I forgot my lunch."

I watched her swish down the hallway with her perfect clothes, perfect shoes, and perfect hair.

"Crap!" I said under my breath, angry that I had to lie.

CHAPTER TWENTY-SIX

A fire glowed in the fireplace from across the room, where we gathered around the big farm table in Joey's kitchen. The spoonful of real butter that Joey's dad plopped on the mounded bowl of steaming mashed potatoes melted and drizzled into the valleys. Mom helped Mrs. McLagan carry the rest of the side dishes. Every Thanksgiving, the spread of ham, roasted turkey, sweet potatoes smothered in marshmallows, corn from last year's gardens, and homemade rolls, somehow looked even better than the year before.

After the moms were seated, it was time to give thanks. We started this tradition years ago, so we began going around the table taking turns. Joey's dad went first.

"Lord, You've gotten us through another year of ranching, provided us with healthy cattle, and blessed us with these here friends to help us along the way. We thank You."

We all nodded and smiled.

Joey's mom cleared her throat. "Good Father, thank You for all the love in this room. With our family so far away, these dear friends have become family to us."

Mom reached across Joey and squeezed his mom's hand.

"Thanks, God, for all this food. I sure am hungry!" Joey winked at his mom, and we all laughed.

Mom looked around the table, then closed her eyes. "Father, we've had quite a hard year, but I've a lot to be thankful for. I pray that you stick around to keep me on the right track. Please bless my family and our host family. I love 'em all," she prayed and then turned to hug me.

I prayed nervously. "Dear God, thank You for everyone here and for all You do for us. And thank You that my parents decided to keep Montana Sky. He's really gonna help cheer us all up."

"Dear Lord, we thank You for taking care of these two kids; for giving them each other's company on a sometimes lonely ol' ranch. Thank You for blessing us with neighbors like family and for keeping us healthy in the years to come." Dad squeezed my hand, looked around the table, and we all said, "Amen."

Joey thought he was being sneaky when he slowly pulled the turkey platter in front of him. But I saw him.

With a confused look on his face, he said, "So, here's my plate. What did you make for the rest of you to eat?"

CHAPTER TWENTY-SEVEN

Normally, we'd be covered in snow by now, but it was a warm day for early December. The fences around the ranch had become weathered from the wet and windy fall. My parents and I loaded the trailer with tools and supplies to spend our Saturday making fence repairs. Mom and I raced over the hill on four-wheelers, leaving Dad behind towing the trailer. My cheeks felt numb from the cold air. The horses watched from what was left of the lower pasture.

Sadie and her foal nuzzled each other inside their separate penned area. When Sadie stepped away, Montana Sky clung by her side. In the pasture holding the mares, where we had stopped, Josie was definitely the dominant horse. I heard heavy neighing when the geldings got too close to the fence, separating them from the mares. Josie stomped and lunged at Slugger

Sam. "Josephina's Pride, you sure are the queen, aren't you?" I laughed.

The sound of thundering hooves made me look up from my fencing. Josie reared up on her back legs, kicking the air. She came down and galloped away followed by Molly and Kiwi. The wind whipped their manes and tails into the air. I always thought that made them look strong and proud. I never got tired of watching the horses running together. Across the fence, the geldings had joined in, running and tossing their heads, like they were flirting with the girls. Island Guy, Izzy for short, ran past with his black coat gleaming, followed by Dragonfly. I was so glad that he was now included in the herd. Since I'd been feeling so much happier, I'd had to flipflop his training and make myself think back to frustrating times when I worked with him. Then, when he began to get upset, I would change my mood to the way I'd been feeling lately—actually happy—and reassure him that he was safe. It was going to take time before he learned not to be so afraid of what he sensed from people, but he was slowly improving. I watched a little longer before getting back to work, grabbing one end of a top rail board Momma was getting from the trailer.

"Dr. Sawyer asked about you at my last session, Kye."

"Yeah?"

"He's found a support group between here and the city that he wants me to try out. A lot of the people come from Billings, but ranchers from surrounding towns come, too. I guess some people drive an hour to get there."

"Wow." I held the end steady, as Mom nailed it to the post, then we moved to the other end to secure it. The lower wire rails needed tightened, so I crimped the wire that Mom held tight.

"I'd like for you and Dad to come with me."

The pliers froze in my hand. I scooted around with my back to Mom and sat on the cool ground. "But Momma-"

"I know. It sounds really uncomfortable. It'll be hard for me, too, to walk into a room full of strangers." She walked around and sat on the ground facing me. "But it's a meeting for family support. There should be other family members there also."

"I...I don't know."

"If you would just go one time, just this once, Kylie, then I'll never ask you to go again."

"Maybe. I'll think about it. Is Dad going?"

"Yep."

As if she knew I needed a distraction, Kiwi plodded over to the fence, peeked her muzzle between the wires, and snorted a steamy hello.

A week later, I sat on my bed, staring in the mirror at my sulking face. I watched Mom trek in and out of the bathroom a million times, getting ready for the support group. I've never seen Momma so nervous. Dad mapped out a route to the small town. Doc told Mom it took some people a long time to start feeling better, and some people found the right combination of medicine quickly. *Thank you, God, Momma is so lucky. Will the people who will be at this meeting be like Momma?*

The meeting was in a church at the edge of a small town. Cars were crammed into the gravel church lot. I walked slowly, checking out everything from luxury SUVs to rusty, rundown pickups. When I got out of the car, the cold air made me shiver.

Mom motioned to the bikes tossed in the frozen dead grass. "I guess there are some local people here."

Inside, the warm room had a damp, musty odor mingled with the smell of brewing coffee. Chairs were spread around the room. People were gathered around the coffee pot and in small groups. A bald man in a flannel shirt, wearing a nametag with "Fred," came over to greet us. He made us nametags and pulled out chairs for us. Finally, people began to find chairs and scoot them around into crooked rows.

"Let's begin our meeting with a prayer," Fred said.

While heads were bowed, I peeked around, studying each person, trying to see something wrong with them. Trying to figure out who was sick and who was just along for the ride, like I was. There were four kids around my age. *Are they sick?*

During the meeting, I sat with my mouth twisted. I bit the inside of my cheek and listened, as people shared their stories. The stories sounded a lot like what happened in my family. Some were not as bad, but some were worse. The kids at this meeting had a manic-depressive parent like me. I watched them closely when their parents spoke. Their heads were up looking at their parents with love, and they smiled at the people's comments. There was no shame, no embarrassment. I remembered my fear that kids would find out about Mom's sickness. I sat up straight and looked around the room at all the people, at Momma. They were all just people—normal people.

I pretended to scratch the corner of my eye to catch a tear before anyone saw it.

I didn't know what to call what I felt. Then one word came to me—peace.

The doors creaked open. A woman stood in the doorway, but she was turned away, whispering to the girl behind her. I watched until they came inside. My eyes widened when I recognized them. My heart did a few flops before I slowly and quietly scooted back my chair, so I could hide behind Mom.

"I'm sorry we're late," the woman said, scrambling to find chairs, avoiding the faces that watched with care.

I peeked around Mom just enough, so I could see.

"He's gone again," the mother said, biting her quivering lip.

A man patted her shoulder, and a woman hugged the girl who had stared at the ground since they came inside. Still, I knew just who she was.

"We suspected he was off his meds. I tried to get him to go see the doctor or to call one of you. I know he's fine. He always comes back. But the not knowing. It's hard."

Oh, God, I had no idea.

I jumped when Mom spoke up. All the eyes in the room looked right at us.

"We're new here. The reason I'm here is that I have bipolar. We're doing okay...now. But it sure is nice to know you are all here if we need you. It's nice to know we're not alone."

The meeting time was almost over before I got the nerve to look again at the people who came in late. They both nodded when our eyes locked, and I nodded back. After the meeting was over, Mom whispered to me, "I'm going to say hi. You can wait here if you want."

I could have sat there and avoided them, or I could have asked Dad to take me to the car. But I remembered the sadness in their eyes when they had arrived. "No. I'll come too."

I smiled at her mom, and then walked up to Olivia. "I didn't know. I'm sorry."

"No one at school knows. When I saw you come out of Mrs. Welling's office, I was only going to tell you that I meet with her, too." She smoothed her silky hair before she went on. "I didn't know your mom was sick. I'm sorry, too."

Dad must have sensed the awkwardness because just in time he came and asked if we were ready to go. I was so relieved that I wanted to hug him.

CHAPTER TWENTY-EIGHT

In the hallway after the bell rang, I found Joey extra annoying. He kept reaching around me, tapping my shoulder to get me to look. When that didn't work, he pulled a curl of my hair straight down my back. "Boing!"

"Don't you have something to do, like maybe go get a haircut? How do you even see where you're going?" I asked.

"Did the meeting go okay last night?" Joey asked.

"It's weird; after last night, it's like I'm starting to get okay. I mean, I still wish she wasn't sick. But it's all right." I stopped and shifted my books to the other arm. "I can't believe that just the other day, I was so embarrassed and ashamed. Something about seeing other people, other kids, with problems like ours. I don't know what happened; it just did. Weird, huh?"

"Yeah, you're weird," Joey said.

"Hey!" I shoved him. "Okay, gotta go see Mrs. Welling. Bye."

I ducked into Mrs. Welling's office and filled her in on the meeting that I went to with my parents.

"I'm so proud of you for going with your mom. Will you be going back?" Mrs. Welling asked.

"I think so. They meet once a month, and they gave Mom names and numbers she can call in case she ever needs to talk. I almost don't care if anyone knows anymore, Mrs. Welling. In fact, I'd like to scream it down the hall: 'Look, this is my mom. This is what crazy looks like! She looks just like your moms, right? What's the big, fat deal?'"

"Why don't you? Not like that, of course. But you— if you are brave enough—you could really take the stigma away from mental illnesses for the kids. You know, solve their mystery and help them understand."

"Well, I guess I was just kidding. Kind of. Maybe not though. Maybe I could do something. But not yet. It's easy to say that I don't care who knows, to you, but not to really say it to my friends."

That night, I lay awake for hours, imagining what I would say in front of my class. Something kept tugging at my heart. I couldn't shake the feeling. "Is that You, God?" I said to the ceiling. "I meant to thank You for the team You chose for me. Since now I see I'm not too good at being captain, if You don't mind , I'm gonna let You be Captain. And if You'll speak really loudly, I'll try really hard to listen. Night, God." I yawned, stretched, then snuggled into the blankets.

CHAPTER TWENTY-NINE

The first morning sun shone a path through the open doors of the stable. It beamed along the dirt floor, then up the side of the straw stacked against the wall. It made the stable feel like it was filled with glowing warmth, even though the temperature had been below freezing for a long time, and it was anything but warm in there. "I have three more stalls to muck before I get ready for school. I better hurry, guys," I told my horses.

Dust from my work glistened in the sunbeam. The horses snorted puffs of steam from their nostrils. This was the last day before the school break. I would probably have extra schoolwork to catch up on during the break, but I was still looking forward to it.

Throughout Christmas break, I thought of Olivia often, and I wondered how she stayed in such an annoyingly good mood all the time. It must be awful not knowing where her dad was. At least when

Momma disappeared, I always knew where she was—usually in her room sleeping.

It wasn't going to be easy, but I needed to do something. I pulled the school directory from the desk drawer, and I dialed Olivia's number to invite her over to share training tips for our barrel race.

When she arrived, as soon as she came inside, Olivia told us that her dad was home, and doing all right. I bundled up, and then we headed out for the stable. She was quieter than usual, so I tried to make up for it by telling her all about the horses.

"I've been training really hard, whenever it's nice enough. I don't think I can win again. I still can't believe I won last year." Olivia paused and rubbed Kiwi's nose. "You are the best rider, Kylie—"

"I know, I know, Olivia. I just barely lost," I tried hard to say it jokingly. "You've reminded me a million times."

"I only wanted you to know that I didn't deserve to beat you. I mean, you're the best rider around here. I thought if you knew it was just luck, you wouldn't be mad at me." Olivia pulled a carrot she'd brought from her coat pocket, held it up, and asked, "Can I feed it to Kiwi?"

When I nodded, Kiwi crunched the tip of the carrot off, and Olivia went on. "But I needed something good to happen to me then. My dad had been really bad. He used to get angry when he had episodes. Me winning that race gave him something to like about me." She offered the rest of the carrot to Kiwi, who waited patiently as always.

I remembered how I prayed for Momma to take some interest in training Dragonfly with me, and after that, the foal. When neither of those worked, I was sure Kiwi's barrel racing would get her to notice me again. I realized Olivia and I had things in common after all. "But it wasn't just luck, Olivia. You deserved to win that race. And I hope your dad noticed."

Dragonfly bumped against the wall, and I knew he had tried to make himself disappear into the corner of the stall.

"Do you think you would want to help me with something?" I asked Olivia.

When she agreed, I explained to her about Dragonfly's sensitivity. I shared how I had been working to desensitize him to the vibes he picked up from people.

"His sensitivity is what will make him a great horse, so I just want to help him learn to calm himself."

Olivia was the perfect person to help me with him. After all, she had all the emotions trapped inside her that I did—maybe even more.

"Can I tell you something kind of weird?" I asked.

"Sure."

"I think Dragonfly is teaching me more about calming myself than I am teaching him."

As if on cue, both of our arms reached up to pet him at the exact same time.

We spent the rest of the day working with Dragonfly and sharing racing tips. I finally had to ask her what had been bothering me. "How could you have been making fun of the lunch lady when your dad is sick?"

She turned quickly and said, "I told you. I didn't."

"But I heard you."

"You didn't hear me. All I did was sit there and turn probably ten shades of red, wondering if people talk about my dad like that. I finally told him to stop and turned away. But then he just went on and on to someone else."

I thought back to that day. "I'm sorry. Now that I think of it, I don't remember you agreeing with him. After that, I worried people would talk about my mom the same way, too."

The day went fast, and before we knew it, it was already time for her to go home. For the first time, I looked forward to seeing Olivia at the locker next to mine after the holidays. I wouldn't even mind hearing her screeching, "Ky-leeee!"

CHAPTER THIRTY

I tucked my birthday shirt into my new jeans, and then polished my silver belt buckle. Mom fastened my two French braids at the ends with blue ribbons, then she rushed up the stairs.

"Here, Kye, wear this," she said on her way back down the stairs, holding out a tube of pale pink lipstick.

"No way, it's a rodeo, not a beauty pageant."

"I know, I know. Just a little for a picture. You look so beautiful!"

I took the tube to the mirror, dabbed on a tiny bit of color to my pale lips, then pinched my cheeks. It worked, now they matched my lips. I backed up to get a full view in the mirror, and I was not sure I knew this young lady in the reflection. The corners of my painted mouth turned up to smile at myself. In the mirror, I saw Dad behind me, shaking his head.

"What? What's wrong?" I asked.

"Wow. You sure look pretty."

I grinned and gave him a hug.

"Now, everyone over here. I'll set the timer for the picture," Dad said as he pushed the button and ran back to get between me and Momma. "Cheese!"

We arrived at the fairgrounds behind Joey's family and their horse trailer. Joey was signed up for calf roping on Butch. I stopped at the side of the trailer where Kiwi waited. "You're always such a patient girl. You timed great at our last practice. I'm sure you're the best horse here. Yes, I am." She stuck her velvety nose against the barred window, so I could pet her. I said goodbye. then I followed Joey up to the registration table.

It was 8:30, and the first event started at 10:00, so we headed to the back of Mr. Riley's indoor arena for breakfast. Every year, Mr. Riley's neighbor set up his catering truck outside the back doors. He cooked up the best breakfast and sold it super cheap.

"Smells good!" I told him.

"Good morning," he said, then he looked to Joey. "Uh oh, sure hope I made enough eats. I see you brought your vacuum along."

"Ha! Look out. He's hungry this morning, too. How many participants this year? Have you heard?" I asked.

"Mr. Riley said there were forty-five entries."

"Mom said five years ago there were only six entries. Wow! Mr. Riley's doing well."

He handed us our plates of steaming biscuits and gravy over potatoes. Joey wasted no time digging in.

I watched Joey shove his last fork, overstuffed with biscuits and gravy, into his mouth. "You pig! You're done already?" I showed him my still full plate.

"Not yet. I'm going back for more."

He actually got back into the food line for more! I thought he was only kidding. When I saw Olivia and her parents sitting with their breakfast, I was so glad to see her dad had come. She noticed me and of course yelled, "Heyyyyy, Ky-leeee!"

"Have a great race, Olivia!" I yelled back. I remembered not to wish her luck since she had thought she just got lucky last year.

We listened to Mr. Riley's announcements over the loudspeaker. "Well, this is what you've all worked so hard for, all year long. I wish everyone the best. I'm sure the news has gotten around. But just in case you haven't heard, thanks to my friends in Texas—we have a new cash prize this year. The first prize winners of all events will evenly split a cash prize of ten thousand dollars!" The crowd broke out in cheers and clapping. "And don't worry, as always, we have some great prizes for second and third places, too. So, let's begin!

A part of ten thousand dollars! I had to take deep breaths to calm down after that news. I had heard a cash prize was being offered this year, but I had no idea it was that big!

We found a good spot to watch the early events. After the bronco event, Joey said, "Let's go get a snack before the calf roping."

"You're kidding right? You just ate two plates of food an hour ago! You can't be hungry. It's just not possible," I said.

Joey gave me a wounded puppy, one eye covered with hair look.

"All right, all right. Let's go," I said. We passed Olivia. "We'll be right back. This poor boy's half starved to death." I rolled my eyes and squeezed past.

The thought of Joey jostling around on his horse with all that food inside of him worried me. When the time came, I promised to root for him and not the calf. Not out loud, anyway. I had to root for the calf, even over Joey. I couldn't help it. They just looked so innocent.

I sat with my parents, behind Joey's parents. The horn blew, and the confused calf trotted into the arena. He took a few steps, then stopped to look around and sniff the ground. He wandered over to the crowd and crossed the score line, giving Joey the signal to come after him. Joey sprang from the stall on Butch with his lasso already in the air before the dazzled calf leapt to a run. Barely in the middle of the arena, Joey had it roped. He dismounted and wrestled it down to get it hogtied with his piggin' string. Butch kept the rope taut for the six seconds before the clock could stop.

"Nine point two seconds!" the announcer called, and the crowd cheered.

"Go, Joey! YAY!" we cheered.

I left to go congratulate Joey. I paused at the calf pen. "Okay you guys, listen up. When the gate opens, run like heck. You hear me now? No messing around checking out the crowd and all—just run!"

The other ropers finished, and Joey had the winning time by two seconds.

"Yay, you won!" I hugged Joey. "That gets you part of the cash prize! Let's see, you just won twenty-five hundred dollars, Joey!"

I took Kiwi outside to warm her up during the break before the barrel races. Olivia was coming inside after her warmup. "Hey, you'll be great. See you after!" I told her.

There was no snow yet, but the wind froze my cheeks, so just a few times around the pasture would have to do. Back in the stall, I rubbed down Kiwi's legs and brushed her, then quickly cinched the saddle one last time. No way was I making that mistake again—especially not today.

"You know what to do, Kiwi. You're a pro at this. Maybe we'll even take first place. Olivia's here racing Harley again this year. And then there's Poker Pete. Out of all the entries, those two are the only two we need to worry about. But you can beat both. No worries, girl."

When my turn arrived, I prayed, *Lord, we could sure use Your help getting around these barrels without falling.*

The flag dropped. Kiwi and I flew down the straightway. I grabbed the saddle horn, as we rounded the first barrel perfectly. Kiwi knew the routine and dug in at the second turn, cutting close but clearing the barrel. I let out my breath and braced for the next barrel. It's just a barrel. You can do this. I pushed the memory of my fall out of my mind, so I only heard the thunder of Kiwi's hooves throwing dirt clods up behind her. "Yes!' I shouted when we cleared the last barrel. I leaned in and kicked her sides with both legs. "Go, go, go!"

Kiwi responded and sprinted to the finish line.

I waved my hat at the crowd as I rode off the arena. "Good girl, Kiwi. We did it, girl!"

"Yeah!" Joey screamed, "Go, Ky-lee!"

My parents met me with congratulation hugs. Then they helped me put Kiwi away, so we could go watch the rest of the racers.

"Come on, come on, you're missing it! You're ahead so far!" Joey said. "Olivia's up next."

Olivia and Harley ran a great race. I found her parents in the crowd. Her dad was standing, waving his hat in the air, cheering her on.

"What's the time? What's the time?" I asked Joey.

"Hang on, Kye. I couldn't hear it. They'll announce in a minute," Joey yelled over the cheering crowd.

Finally, the announcer called over the loudspeaker, "We have a tie! So far, Kylie on Kiwi and Olivia on Harley are tied for first place! But wait, we have one more rider before we know the winner!"

Joey and I said at the same time, "A tie?" We turned to watch Poker Pete charge out after the horn blew. He was fast this year, flying between the barrels, but his turns seemed wide. That had to cost him. Poker Pete's time was close, but it didn't beat mine or Olivia's.

Mr. Riley took the microphone. "Well, a tie! Hadn't counted on that, had we?"

The crowd broke out in cheers.

"I said we'd split the first-place prize evenly between the winners. But I know you've all done the math already. That wouldn't be fair to give you all a fifth instead of a fourth of that ten-thousand dollars, now would it?"

The arena cheers died off. Across the crowd, I caught the worried look on Olivia's face. We were both wondering the same thing. Would one of us not be a first-place winner?

"Hmm. Let me think about this. Hmm, here's an idea," Mr. Riley continued. "How about I add another twenty-five hundred to the prize to make it fair?"

The crowd went nuts! My mouth dropped, and Olivia and I rushed through the people to hug each other. "We both won first place, Olivia! We did it!"

She was jumping up and down squealing. I saw him coming, so I stepped back to let her dad close. He grabbed her and gave her the biggest hug.

My knees shook all the way back to where Joey waited for me. "Joey, did I really just win $2500? Really? I never thought I would say this, but pinch me, will you? Because I am so afraid this is a dream!"

CHAPTER THIRTY-ONE

Thank God, things at home with Momma kept improving. After the rodeo, I had an idea. But when I read every article I could find and realized there would be a million details that all seemed impossible, I'd finally given up on my dream. But all week, the idea kept popping back into my head. Why would God keep reminding me of this? All it did was make me sad and grumpy.

Just then, the picture taped to the back of my bedroom door stopped me cold. "Well, duh!" I jerked the door open. "Mom! Dad! Can we invite Joey and his folks over for dinner tonight? Please!"

That evening, I helped Mom roll out the dough for the homemade beef and noodles. I sliced them thin, the way Mom taught me, and then began peeling potatoes. At the other end of the table, Mom scooped big globs of chocolate chip cookie dough onto a baking sheet. After dinner, while the cookies were still warm, they would be topped with vanilla ice cream, whipped topping, and chocolate syrup. My mouth watered just thinking about our favorite dessert.

The McLagans arrived, and they all sat with Dad at the table. Out the dining room window, the moon glistened against a blanket of fresh snow. As we ate, the house filled with the sweet smell of fresh-baked cookies.

Joey must have sensed that I was up to something. I could tell by the way he watched me shovel down my dinner. I wanted to wait until dessert, which I thought would never come. I knew I couldn't keep this idea inside much longer.

Mom and I brought out dessert and cups of coffee. Finally, Mom sat down, so I took a deep breath. The words started flying from my mouth so fast. If I had wanted to, I wouldn't have been able to stop them. "I really want to tell everyone about an idea I have! I have read up on it, and I know it's quite a big dream, and I was just going to forget it! But today, I saw this picture from the year Joey and I went to church camp."

I held up the picture for them to see. We looked so small standing on each side of the basketball player, who was the speaker. His huge hands were on our shoulders, covering most of our arms. We were rosy faced and all grins. I remembered his great smile, and his words rang in my head. "He had the best message; I'll never forget it. 'Ya can't do everything on your own now. God'll send you a team, and you work together with your team. Tell me, who's the captain?' I remembered how we all joined to yell, 'God!'"

"The picture reminded me that God already sent me my team."

The way they all glanced at each other around the table, I could tell they were confused. "Mom, remember your dream to start a horse rescue at our ranch? And remember you telling me about how now that you are getting treatment, the horses make you feel better, calmer?"

Mom nodded her head.

"Why couldn't we turn our ranch into a therapeutic riding ranch? That way, you could help other people with problems to feel better, too. Then, maybe you could also rescue horses and train them to be therapy horses!"

Mom's face brightened, as she thought for a minute. "You know, Kylie, I always think of therapeutic ranches for physical rehab. I never thought of one for mental or emotional therapy."

"I know, me either! But there was an article about it in a magazine at doc's. I read it while we waited for you," I told her.

"You're right though. It's quite a big dream. But wouldn't it be great to use my work with horses to help others? I love it! It's perfect for us."

"Momma, we have the horses. We have trails and a round pen," I added.

Dad raised his hand like he was in school. "I don't mean to stomp on your dreams, really. But this idea would cost A LOT of money. I don't want you to get your hopes up."

"We could use my prize money! The whole $2500! I know that's not enough. But we can't just give up; we might be able to do it someday?"

"Sounds like we got some serious praying to do!" Joey's mom reached out for hands, and all heads bowed to pray.

CHAPTER THIRTY-TWO

Time passed, and nothing but bad news came when we tried to get the money for the therapeutic riding ranch. Between licensing, insurance, special equipment, and training, the start-up costs were rocket high. Tonight, I couldn't even sleep. Giving up the therapeutic ranch idea made me cry, even though I had promised Dad that I wouldn't get up my hopes. I rubbed the tears off my cheeks and shoved my hands into the air. "I give up, God! We can't do it. We tried, but we just can't do it without You! You're supposed to be the Captain!"

When Mom and I unloaded the dishwasher the next day, we heard a knock at the door. "Huh. Wonder who that is? Too early for Joey," I said.

Mr. Riley waited outside, dressed in his imported leather trench coat over one of his fine suits. He came inside, and as he talked, I listened closely to his words, trying to take them all in. First, I was confused, then my fists clenched, and finally my mouth dropped open in shock. All along my heart raced faster than Mr. Riley's fastest thoroughbred. *Did he just say what I think he said?*

"You mean it, Mr. Riley? You really mean it?" I asked, close to shaking.

Mr. Riley smiled a slow smile. "I mean it, Kylie. Every word. I'm sponsoring you enough money to start up your riding program and to pay the first three years running costs. And we can't have you closing down during our long winters."

"That's what I thought you said!" I ran to him. "Thank you! Thank you!" I hugged him so hard I knocked off his hat, sending it flying from his head.

I turned to Momma, who hugged me, lifting me off the ground. Then she spun me around the living room. "I can't believe it!"

"Me neither, Sunshine!" Mom said.

Mr. Riley went on, "I called my friends in Texas and told them what your mom told me about your dream. At the rodeo, they got a taste of what a great community we have here. And they were pretty impressed with all of the event winners. So, they decided it would be a good investment to make. They're in, too!"

"Oh my gosh. I better sit down," I said, fanning my face with my hand.

"Well, don't sit long. You've got a lot of work to do, Missy," Mr. Riley teased on his way out. "Meet me at my house, Monday. We'll take care of the paperwork."

When the door closed, I shouted, "I've gotta call Joey!"

Mom cupped my face in her hands and kissed my forehead. "Go, go, hurry!"

I shot upstairs, like my jeans were on fire to get to the phone.

"Joey! Joe! You're not gonna believe this. You are just not gonna believe it! I'm still not sure I believe it!"

"What? Kylie, slow down. I can barely understand you," Joey shouted.

"Okay, listen, are you listening?" I took a breath. "Someone knocks at the door, right? I go, and there stands Mr. Riley, all spiffied up like he gets, Beemer parked out front and all. So, I tell him to come in, and I holler for Momma, right?"

"Yeah, right," Joey was getting impatient.

"So, he said he doesn't want to talk to Mom; he wants to talk to me.

"And I'm thinking, oh crap, what'd I do now? So, Mom walked in, and he said to me, he said, 'So Miss Kylie, you ready to start tearing down that barn out there?'

"I musta looked at him like he lost his stinking mind, cause that's just what I was thinking. I mean, what kinda question is that to ask someone, huh?" I breathed again. "So, I said, 'Tear down the what?' and Mr. Riley, he didn't smile or nothing.

"Finally, he said, 'Well, you're wanting to start a therapeutic riding ranch here. Is that right?' he asked me. I'm so confused. I can't figure out why he would want to tear down our barn!"

"What the heck?"

"Then you know what he said next, Joey?"

"What'd he say?"

"He said, 'Seems to me the only way for me to build you a new indoor riding arena is to first tear down that barn.' And then it hits me. He's serious! He's going to pay for an INDOOR ARENA for us! Can you believe it? Did you hear me? He said Mom was working with his horse, Shotzie, the other day. She told him we'd decided to give up on the ranch. He told her, 'No way!' He loved the idea! He's even donating more money to help us get started. I seriously thought I was gonna crap right there, Joey. I'm still in shock!"

"Are you for real? Go, Mr. Riley! That's great! I got more news for you, but I can't tell you. We're coming over later," Joey said.

"You're kidding? Maybe it's good you can't tell me. I don't think I could take any more news, of any kind, right now."

Later, from the upstairs window, I spotted Joey's truck turning onto our lane. "Mom, the McLagans are here. They're pulling their trailer," I yelled down the stairs. "What are they doing?" I asked, hopping on one foot, trying to get my boots on.

Dad came up from the shed and met them in the driveway. "Come on, Momma. Let's see what's up."

We got there in time to see Joey lead a calf down the trailer ramp.

"What are you doing?" I asked.

"We figured there was a reason Senorita had twins this year. Mom and Dad decided to give this girl to you guys. She comes from prize-winning stock. The price she'll bring can go toward the ranch."

I stood with my mouth hanging wide open, couldn't say a thing.

Senorita's calf made a bawling sound.

"And Joey has a great idea," his mom said. "He thinks we ought to get together with the other ranchers and see if they'd want to have a Calf-a-Thon! Ask them if they'd be willing to donate one of their calves as a tax write-off. The money from their sale would be a benefit for your ranch."

Finally, I found the words to say with my voice trembling, "For our ranch," before I choked on the tears that I couldn't hold in one more minute.

Mom put her arm around me. "There's more. Mr. Jinks was so impressed at how far you've come with Dragonfly. He's donating him to the program! He thinks a horse that sensitive will make a great therapy horse someday, and he trusts that you'll train him well."

After swallowing the huge lump in my throat, I said, "You know, that God, He's something else. He just kinda hangs around and waits with his game plan. Waits for you to finally figure out you can't do things on your own, and for you to let Him be the Captain. Then, bam!"

"Yeah, bam!" Joey shoved my shoulder.

"A Calf-a-Thon. Pretty smart idea, Joe." I wiped at my nose, kicked at the tire, then awkwardly hugged Joey. "Thanks."

I looked forward to my next meeting with Mrs. Welling at school.

"Kylie, I'm so happy for you all! I'd love to volunteer once a month for now and more when I can," Mrs. Welling told me in her office after hearing my good news. "I understand Dr. Jordan will be retiring this year and plans to work with your groups weekly."

"Yeah, it's great, isn't it? We've got a real team." I looked at Mrs. Welling for a moment, gathering my courage. "Mrs. Welling, there's one more thing I need to take care of before the end of the school year and before the word of our ranch starts getting around. But I'm going to need your help."

CHAPTER THIRTY-THREE

As I stepped out onto the stage before the sixth, seventh, and eighth graders at Smithson Junior High, I lifted my eyes and thought, "Okay, Captain. Here goes."

My notes were clenched in my fist, and I was afraid my voice would crack because of my desert dry mouth. I scanned my audience seeing only a blur. Come on, relax. When the crowd slowly came into focus, I thanked God for sending me to such a small school. Because with one more row of faces, I'd surely chicken out. In the front row, Mrs. Welling sat with a reassuring smile on her face. She nodded to me as if to say, "You can do this."

On her right, the boys who talked about the lunch lady elbowed each other, then they pointed at me and whispered. I pulled my eyes away when I felt like a tiny team of gymnasts were inside my stomach competing in the Olympics. My eyes landed on Olivia, sitting perfectly straight in her perfect clothes. She stared at me with her perfect smile. But now I knew that her life was far from perfect. I smiled back. I was sorry that I had ever been annoyed by her.

I kept searching the crowd. *There he is.* Closer to the front and off to my left, I locked eyes with Joey and winked. Then I began, "Hello, my name is Kylie Hannigan, and I might just go crazy someday. Nice to meet ya."

A hushed giggle filled the room. Some of the kids turned to their friends, and I could read their lips asking, "What?"

I looked back to Joey, who winked and gave me the thumbs up sign. I took a deep breath. "That's what I want to talk about today. Did you know that 56 million people in the U.S. have a mood disorder or a mental illness? Or—you may call them, crazy. When you think of crazy, what do you picture? Maybe you picture this."

I pointed off to my left. Mr. Collins, the principal, entered the stage. His face was covered with white makeup and exaggerated dark circles under his eyes. His hair looked like a porcupine. He flailed his arms like a windmill, and his mouth stretched open like he was screaming, "Ahh!"

The kids laughed.

"Or maybe even this," I added.

I turned to watch Mrs. Cressup, the math teacher, sneak out from behind the corner. She was covered in a hooded shirt, her face also made up to look stark. She saw the crowd then yanked the hood over her face and squirreled back behind the corner. I extended my hand and tried to coax her back onto the stage. Mrs. Cressup crept over almost taking my hand but at the last minute turned and ran away.

"How about this?"

I motioned to the other side of the stage. Mr. Jacobs, the janitor, had dressed in many layers of mismatched clothes. He walked on the stage taking uneven steps, watching the ground while he stepped over things that weren't there.

The kids laughed more.

"We can laugh at this now, because we know Mr. Collins, Mrs. Cressup and Mr. Jacobs." They all stepped forward and bowed. "And we know they really aren't sick."

"But millions and millions and millions of people are. That's a lot of people dealing with a really crappy—I mean—horrible illness. And it's not just them; it's their families—their friends—the people they work with—if they even can work. If we really knew about the confusion they live with every day; and the pain of the people who love them, would we laugh at them? It's nothing to laugh at—really. But we don't want to know about it. It makes us uncomfortable. So, we either look away, or we laugh."

I took another deep, shaky breath.

"I didn't understand mental illness, and I called it crazy. You know, that bad word we use to describe people we don't understand. I've spent this year pretending and hiding, afraid someone would find out that someone I know has a mental illness. Afraid they would call this person crazy, and they'd say I'm gonna be crazy, too. But that was before I learned that mental illness is a sickness. I learned I have nothing to be ashamed of."

I paused and swallowed hard when I saw my dad, off to the side, wipe a tear from his eye. "Look around you. Remember that the crazy man you're talking about could be the father of the kid sitting in front of you. His father has an illness. That's all."

I watched the kids shifting around in their places, looking from side to side.

"Very few mental illnesses might look a little like these." I motioned back to my three helpers. "Actually, one third of the people with mental illness look like this."

"This is someone you might have called crazy before." Then, I turned to watch my mom walk onto the stage, looking the prettiest I'd ever seen her. My clenched fists loosened. "This is my mom. She's not crazy."

The room became so quiet I could hear my heart pounding.

"This year, my mom was diagnosed with bipolar disorder. Bipolar is a mood disorder also called manic-depressive."

Mom stepped to the microphone to share the rest of the details of the secret that only months ago had held me like a prisoner.

Slowly, I stepped back with an easy smile on my face. Because the weight on my heart—that had only lately begun to ease—lifted...and disappeared.

.

ACKNOWLEDGEMENTS

There are so many people to thank who helped me in some way with this story:

My mom and dad for loving me and encouraging me in anything I tried; my husband, Greg, for patience and for helping me with word choices now and then; the very first readers–my cousin Darcy, my cousin Christie (RIP), my Aunt Kay, my friend Sherri; the two ladies who had barely met me, Dawn and Mary, who sent me pages of wonderful, helpful notes on my awful first draft.

I also want to thank my writers' group: Margo, Fred, Darcy, Brenda, Clyde and Terrill (and the others who came and went along the way)- who taught me so much. I enjoyed every second of our meetings!

Then there's Bev, for convincing me to save a third of this story for another book; my cousin Teresa for her final edits and great suggestions; Martie, for letting me spend time with her horses and letting me drink up her horse senses; Jamey, for posing for my cover; Jama for photographing her horse, Cowboy, and getting just the right angle I needed; Louann, for offering a helpful critique on the front cover; cousins Martha and Keith for tips about raising cattle; my sweet editor/publisher, Margo Dill, for loving Kylie's story enough to publish it!

And most importantly, thank You, God, for everything great in my life and for sending me all of these people when I needed them so much.

ABOUT THE AUTHOR

Cinda Bauman lives in Central Illinois with her husband and dogs. During her high school years, she took every art class offered along with every child development class. After a class where she spent part of the day at a daycare, child development won out over art. Years of story time led to a love of children's picture-books, which made her wish she had stuck with art.

Flash forward to today, and she still loves children's books! After researching and much study; learning about writing and illustrating children's books, she joined the Society of Children's Book Writers and Illustrators (SCBWI) and found her passion. Besides writing children's picture books and middle-grade novels, Cinda also creates with cut paper sculptures and paints in oil and acrylic. She loves iris flowers and the color purple.

Only My Horses Know is her debut middle-grade novel.

ABOUT THE PUBLISHER

E ditor-911 Books publishes entertaining and informative books for children of all ages and adults, specifically writers and parents. Owned by Margo L. Dill, we are located in St. Louis, MO, and on the web at Editor-911.com. The three imprints under Editor-911 Books are Editor-911 Kids, Editor-911 Romance and Editor-911 Knowledge.

To find out when Cinda's next middle-grade novels will be out, you can sign up for our newsletter at Editor-911.com on the Editor-911 Books page to get updates and a free picture ebook, *Maggie Mae, Detective Extraordinaire: The Case of the Missing Cookies*, delivered right to your inbox!

Other books by Editor-911 Kids are:

- *Anna and the Baking Championship*, middle-grade historical fiction, by Margo L. Dill

Editor-911 Books
Books for Readers of All Ages
Imprints:
Editor-911 Kids
Editor-911 Knowledge
Editor-911 Romance

- *Finding My Place: One Girl's Strength at Vicksburg* (ebook format, print book by White Mane Kids), middle-grade historical fiction, by Margo L. Dill

- *Read-Aloud Stories with Fred Vol. 1: Three Bedtime Stories in One Book*, read-aloud children's stories, by Fred Olds

- *Read-Aloud Stories with Fred Vol. 2: Three Anytime Stories in One Book*, read-aloud children's stories, by Fred Olds

- *The Dog and the Flea: A Tale of Two Opposites*, picture book, text by Fred Olds, illustrations by Robert T. Tong

- *That's the Way It Always Happened*, picture book, text by Margo L. Dill, illustrations by Pamella Withroder

Made in the USA
Monee, IL
23 February 2021

61220671R00118